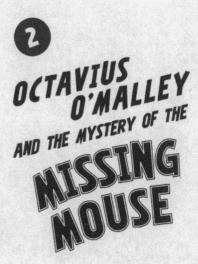

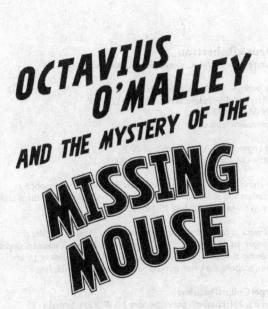

OCTAVIUS O'MALLEY AND THE MYSTERY OF THE MISSING MOUSE

ALAN SUNDERLAND

Angus&Robertson
An imprint of HarperCollins*Children's*Books

Angus&Robertson
An imprint of HarperCollins *Children's Books*, Australia

First published in Australia in 2007
by HarperCollins*Publishers* Australia Pty Limited
ABN 36 009 913 517
harpercollins.com.au

HarperCollins*Publishers*
Level 13, 201 Elizabeth Street, Sydney NSW 2000, Australia
Unit D1, 63 Apollo Drive, Rosedale, Auckland 0632, New Zealand
A 53, Sector 57, Noida, UP, India
1 London Bridge Street, London SE1 9GF, United Kingdom
2 Bloor Street East, 20th floor, Toronto, Ontario M4W 1A8, Canada
195 Broadway, New York NY 10007, USA

National Library of Australia Cataloguing-in-Publication data:

Sunderland, Alan, 1959– .
   Octavius O'Malley and the mystery of the missing mouse.
   For children.
   ISBN 978 0 207 20049 6.
   ISBN 0 207 20049 1.
   1. Mice – Juvenile fiction. I. Title. (Series: Sunderland, Alan,
   Octavius O'Malley; bk. 2).
A823.2

Cover and internal design by Darren Holt, HarperCollins Design Studio
Cover illustration by Ben Redlich
Typeset in 11.5 on 17pt Weiss by HarperCollins Design Studio
Printed and bound in Australia by McPherson's Printing Group
The papers used by HarperCollins in the manufacture of this book are a natural,
recyclable product made from wood grown in sustainable plantation forests. The
fibre source and manufacturing processes meet recognised international
environmental standards, and carry certification.

For Cathy, who taught José
how to speak Spanish

1
JUST ANOTHER DAY

I had the doughnut resting on my knee and my knee resting on the edge of my desk when the red phone rang.

I **hate** it when the red phone rings.

I jumped with surprise, and my knee jerked forward and banged the table, and the doughnut fell on the floor with the chocolate icing face down.

I said, **'Ouch!'** and then I said, **'Oh no!'**, and then I picked up the red phone and said, **'What?'**

There was silence.

I sighed and then I started again, trying to sound a little bit more like a Chief of Police. That is, of course, what I am — the Chief of Police.

'Chief O'Malley here,' I said into the red phone. 'What's happening?'

The red phone only rings when there is an emergency. A **real** emergency. The kind of emergency that needs the brilliant skills and amazing abilities of Octavius O'Malley, the finest policerat in all of Rodent City.

1

'It's an **emergency**, sir ... an **emergency**!'

I immediately recognised the nasal, slightly annoying voice of Deputy Smith, one of my best police officers. Although that's not saying much — they were all a bit thick if you ask me. .

I spoke slowly and patiently into the red phone.

'I **know** it's an emergency, Smith, otherwise you wouldn't be calling on the red phone. Now, take a deep breath and tell me what's going on.'

Deputy Smith took a deep breath, and told me what was going on.

'It's the humans, sir. The monkey people. They've attacked our Number Three Food Store.'

'Don't move, Smith,' I replied. 'I'm on my way.'

I hung up the red phone, grabbed my shiny police badge from the desk in front of me, and leapt to my feet.

It was a fine, bold gesture, and my next plan was to stride out the door looking every inch the brilliant Police Chief that I was. Unfortunately, I stepped right on the dropped doughnut, skidded awkwardly across the room, bounced off the hatstand in the corner, hit the wall and slid heavily down. Then I got up and limped slowly through the door, with crumbs and chocolate icing all over my trousers and my shiny police badge forgotten on the floor. I could see it was going to be one of those days.

Rodent City is a fine town, by and large. Rats are fine folk, although you will always get the occasional troublemaker. The mice are much better than they used to be, too. There was a time when you wouldn't hear me say a good word about mice. When I was a younger policerat, I thought mice were a blight on society, but I know better now. I can live with mice. It's you people I can't stand.

That's right — **you!** Don't pretend you don't know what I'm talking about. You humans, or monkey people as we like to call you, are nothing but trouble. You stomp around the world as if you own it, and when you're not trying to poison us or trap us or experiment on us, you're running around screaming like idiots just because you bump into us on the street. What do you think a rat is going to do to you, anyway — eat you? Honestly.

So keep that in mind next time you are out on the streets of Rodent City — we don't like you any more than you like us. I bet you're sitting there reading this book and thinking, **Oh well, I've never been to Rodent City**. Wrong again! You're probably in Rodent City right now and you don't even know it.

Rodent City is underneath every street and every building in every city in the world. We live right under your nose and most of the time you don't even know it. We have our secret paths, our special ways of getting around unnoticed. If you want to know more about it, then just keep reading, because I'm on my way down one of those secret paths right now, to see what damage you monkey people have done this time.

I was still limping as I left police headquarters and slipped down the nearest drain. Luckily for me, it had been raining recently, so the water in the underground pipe was flowing nicely. No need to walk when the police provide special vehicles for just such an occasion. I unhooked one of the official ice-cream containers tied up to the wall, climbed in and let the current take me downstream about four blocks.

As I reached the intersection with Drain Line Number Sixty-five, I clambered gracefully out of the container and landed flat on my back in the muddy grey water. At least it soaked the last of the crumbs out of my now-sodden trousers. From there it was back up into the street, along the gutter a few metres, and then up a drainpipe into the roof space of an old warehouse. A bit more clambering, a little climbing, a jump or two and a stroll down the space between two brick walls, and I had arrived.

I pushed a fake brick out of the way and walked into the Number Three Food Store. It was not a pretty sight.

Water! Water! A rat raced past me, waving his arms in the air, and calling for water. I looked behind him, and saw a small crowd gathered around someone who was lying on the floor groaning. Then I looked to the left and saw two more groups doing the same thing.

Multiple casualties, I thought to myself. One whole corner of the Food Store had been cordoned off with police tape to keep a crowd of rats and mice away from a pile of boxes that had tumbled over, spilling pellets everywhere.

'Everybody stand clear! Keep away from the food! This area is not secure.' I recognised the voice yelling these instructions through the crowd — it was Deputy Smith. I made my way towards him, but just then I heard a loud **SNAP** from the other side of the room, and someone yelped in pain.

'It's another one! Another one! Stand clear please for your own safety.' called Deputy Smith.

I knew what that snapping sound meant as soon as I heard it. Any rat who has been around Rodent City long enough knows that sound — the sound of a rat-trap being sprung. Your average mouse-trap sounds just like someone snapping their fingers, but a rat-trap is like a clap of thunder, or the crack of a tree branch breaking in a storm.

I could see that everyone was starting to panic, and that Deputy Smith's appeals for calm were, as usual, useless. I reached into the pocket of my police jacket, pulled out my standard-issue whistle, and blew with every ounce of breath I had.

WHHEEEEEEEEEEEETT!!!

Silence. Everyone froze. Even the groaners on the ground stopped groaning for a brief moment. I used that brief moment to take charge. Clambering onto an overturned box, and ignoring the green pellets scattered around me, I spoke in the loudest voice I could muster.

'Okay! Everyone move calmly and slowly to the far side of the room, away from the boxes. Leave the injured where they are — the medics will see to them. There may be more traps hidden around the Food Store, so please stay alert, and don't put your feet down unless you can see where you're putting them. My police officers will want to speak to all of you, so stand by until someone has taken your names.'

The crowd started mumbling, the groaners

resumed their groaning, and the police and ambulance rats went to work. I walked over to Deputy Smith.

'Deputy Smith, work the room. I want a full status report in two minutes. Are there any deaths?'

'No, I don't think so,' said Deputy Smith, 'but I haven't checked out that last trap yet. I'll go and do that now.'

I approached one of the rats lying on the ground groaning. A friend crouched beside him, holding his hand.

'Phil, you're an **idiot**,' said his friend. 'I told you: **don't eat the green stuff. don't eat the green stuff!** What are you, **crazy** or something?'

'I was **hungry**,' said the groaning rat weakly.

'Drink some water,' I said. 'It should help. How much did you eat?'

'Just one pellet,' said the rat on the ground, but his friend interrupted.

'Don't lie, Phil, it was **two**! I saw you scoff the second one even after I told you to stop.'

'I was **hungry**,' said Phil again, then he looked up at me. 'Am I gonna die, Doc?'

'I'm not a doctor, I'm a policerat. You must be delirious. And no, I don't think you'll die, but you can forget about rich food for at least a month. Bread and water for you, and quite frankly it serves you right.'

I can't believe these rats sometimes. No matter how often you tell them about the danger signals, they still go ahead and eat the rat poison. Green pellets! How obvious is **that**? But they still eat them. I guess there's one born every minute.

Last year, as soon as I got the job as Police Chief, I started a public campaign, with leaflets, posters and even fridge magnets. The slogans were great; I made them up myself.

```
If the pellet is green, call police to the
   scene.
Don't eat it or smell it, steer clear of
   the pellet.
If you find some green pellets and decide
   to try your luck, don't blame us if you
   end up a dead duck.
```

The last one was probably a bit long, but I guess I was getting carried away by then.

Just as I was trying to think up a new, even better slogan (what rhymes with poison?), Deputy Smith returned.

'No fatalities, Chief,' he said. 'Three poison victims, but it looks like they'll all survive.'

'What about the traps?' I said.

'Not too bad. Two broken arms, and one tail that will never be the same again.'

'Ouch!' I said. We rats are very proud of our tails.

Leaving Smith and the team to clean up the mess, I strolled back to my office. I rubbed my whiskers thoughtfully and pondered whether this was some sort of new attack by the monkey people or just the usual low-level harassment.

After all, it was a grand plan by the humans to get rid of all the rats that got me involved in my last great adventure. Could it be happening all over again?

I was still lost in thought when I opened the door of

my office and saw a tall, thin mouse with luxuriant black fur leaning casually against the desk, wearing a red waistcoat and green trousers.

'Spencer!' I said.

Spencer was the first mouse I'd ever called a friend, but things had changed. I hadn't laid eyes on her since our last big argument six months ago. What was she doing in my office?

'We've got trouble,' she said, without so much as a hello. **'Big** trouble.'

2
THE MISSING MOUSE

'What do you mean, he's **missing**?' I said.

Spencer sighed.

'Ocko,' she said. 'I mean exactly what I said. **Patrick the Magnificent is missing.** He was there and now he's not.'

'Well, what do you want **me** to do about it?' I snapped.

Spencer snapped straight back. 'Finding him might be a good start. Or are you too important to help your friends these days?'

I leant back in my chair and remembered the days when mice didn't talk to rats like this. Mice were respectful — they knew their place. There used to be a time when no self-respecting rat would be caught dead talking to a mere mouse. And woe betide any mouse who —

'OCKO! Stop daydreaming!'

'I wasn't,' I lied.

'OF course you were,' said Spencer. 'Try to focus on

the problem at hand, Ocko. **Patrick ... is ... missing.** And I need your help.'

Have I mentioned that I am the Chief of Police? That means I have dozens of policerats under my command. Some of them even know what they are doing. I could press a button on my desk right now, and half a dozen of them would come running, ready for the next case to investigate.

But as I sat there staring at Spencer, I knew I wouldn't press that button. This case was special, and it was one I would have to handle myself.

Patrick the Magnificent. Patrick. The Magnificent. The name brought back so many memories. The first time I ever saw him I grabbed him by the ankles, turned him upside down and shook him. Sounds mean, I know, but you have to realise he was holding me prisoner at the time.

Back then, Patrick and Spencer were both members of the notorious River Road Mouse Gang, the worst bunch of mouse crooks in Rodent City, or so I thought. I started out trying to arrest them, but they finished up becoming my best friends, and helping me thwart a fiendish plot to destroy us all. Those were the days ...

'OCKO! Pay attention!'

I realised Spencer had been talking while I was sitting there daydreaming again. So I sat up straight, picked up a pencil, and put on my most serious Police Chief expression (the one where I wrinkle my brow, frown slightly, wag my whiskers and look very, very intelligent).

'Okay, Spencer,' I said. 'Let's start at the beginning.'

I wrote something down on the pad in front of me. It was just the word **Patrick**, but it made me feel like I was getting somewhere.

'Right,' I went on. 'When did you see him last?'

'I just **told** you that!' said Spencer. 'Weren't you listening?'

'**Of course** I was listening. But tell me again anyway.'

'Okay,' said Spencer, 'but could you pay attention this time? It was eight days ago. Like I said, Patrick was trying to break into this safe at the First Rodent Bank —'

'**What??!!**' I spluttered. 'Spencer, I thought we agreed the River Road Mouse Gang's days of crime were over. We talked about this after the Mystery of the Exploding Cheese, and all five of you promised to go straight. You and Patrick and Larry and Garry and Barry —'

'See! I **knew** you weren't listening!' said Spencer triumphantly. 'Patrick was **working** for the bank, testing their security systems. You **know** there's no lock he can't pick, no safe he can't open. So these days lots of companies use him to see how good their locks are. I help him sometimes, when I'm not too busy running the meetings of the Society for the Cooperation of Rats And Mice — remember? Those meetings that you don't bother coming along to any more? And Larry, Garry and Barry work delivering food around Rodent

14

City. I **told** you all this ages ago!'

I'd forgotten how much Spencer likes a good argument.

'Can we get on with this, please?' I said.

Spencer glared at me. 'Patrick was trying to break into this safe, and he'd just got his toothpick and piece of chewing gum right where he wanted them, when one of the bank clerks came into the room and interrupted him. He gave him a note.'

'A note?' I said, writing all of this down.

'A note,' said Spencer. 'The clerk said it was urgent, and it had just been dropped off at the front desk. Patrick had to stop what he was doing, which really annoyed him. He read it, read it a second time, then screwed it up and stuffed it quickly into his waistcoat pocket.'

'**Then** what?' I asked. This was getting interesting.

'Then he turned to me and said, "I've gotta go." And he went.'

'Just like that?' I asked.

'Just like that,' she said.

'No explanation?'

'No explanation.'

'How did he seem when he left?'

Spencer hesitated, looked down and brushed a doughnut crumb from her waistcoat, and then looked at me again.

'He looked scared, Ocko,' she said. '**Really** scared.'

****

Ten minutes later, Spencer and I were sitting in an ice-cream container floating down Drain Line Number Five in the direction of the First Rodent Bank.

I had told Deputy Smith that I was taking an early lunch. After all, I could hardly tell him I was off to try and rescue a member of the River Road Mouse Gang. As far as he and the rest of the Rodent Police Force knew, the gang were desperate criminals who were still wanted for bank robbery, theft from a bakery, and various acts of public mischief. How was he to know I had let them escape from the long arm of the law and start a new life because I **liKed** them?

The First Rodent Bank is just like one of your human banks, except for two important differences. First of all, we don't have those ridiculous automatic teller machines. After all, who wants to trust a machine to look after their money? When **we** go to the bank, we line up and talk to a real live rat, who counts out our money for us and hands it over. Always do business with rats — that's **my** motto.

The second difference is that when we take our money out of the bank, we mostly take out one thing — coins. Never banknotes, only coins. Want to know why? Let me mention two words: vending machines.

What do you think rats do with money, anyway? We can hardly walk into one of your human shops, stroll up to the counter and say: 'Half a kilo of cheese, please.' You'd have a fit. But vending machines — they're a different matter altogether.

At night, when the streets are quiet, we rats go shopping. An empty sack and a handful of gold coins — that's all we need. An hour later we're back home safe and sound with chocolate bars, cheese and crackers, cookies, muesli bars. The other day I even found a vending machine at a train station that sold doughnuts, my personal favourite.

The ice-cream container bumped to a stop against an old sandstone wall. Spencer and I climbed out and walked up a narrow lane to the bank.

Inside, there were three tellers in their little cages, each with a row of customers in front of them waiting to be served. There was also a long counter, and behind it were rows and rows of desks. There were rats counting money, rats scribbling away on pieces of paper, rats adding up numbers with calculators, and rats staring off into space while sucking the ends of pencils. **Bureau-rats**, we call them.

'Recognise anyone?' I said to Spencer.

'Right there,' she said. 'The third desk from the end — the one sucking his pencil. He's the one who gave Patrick the note.'

I looked in the direction that Spencer was pointing,

and I saw the particular bureau-rat we were after. I must admit he looked a little stupid. He was just sitting there, sucking his pencil with a vacant look in his eyes. His whiskers were droopy, his nose was long and spotty, and his tail was most unimpressive. He didn't look like the best witness, but he was all we had.

I walked over and rapped on the counter.

Nothing.

I rapped again, a little louder, and cleared my throat.

Nothing.

Time to let them know who's boss, I thought, reaching for my police badge. Then I realised it wasn't there. I'd left it lying on my office floor. **Rats!**

'Excuse me,' I said loudly, 'this is official police business.'

The rat closest to me looked up, sighed, and got to his feet. He walked over and stared sullenly at me.

'You made me lose count,' he said. 'What do you want?'

'I need to speak to that rat there,' I said, pointing in the direction of the third desk from the end, 'and I would appreciate you getting him for me. **Now**.'

The sullen rat wandered over to the stupid rat, leant down and whispered in his ear. Then the stupid rat, the one we needed to talk to, put down the pencil he'd been sucking and ambled slowly over.

How did anything ever get done in this bank? A rat could die waiting for some service. Finally, the stupid rat arrived at the counter, looked at me as if I had just interrupted his favourite daydream (which I probably had) and said, 'Yes, sir?'

'I am the Chief of Police, Octavius O'Malley,' I said, 'and I need your help.'

That got his attention. He straightened his shoulders, his whiskers stopped drooping, and he smiled.

'My name is Oliver Drong. How can I help you?'

'Well, Oliver, are you familiar with a mouse by the name of Patrick? He has been working here recently, testing your security equipment.'

Oliver Drong's smile got a little wider.

'You mean the little guy who uses a toothpick and chewing gum to bust open our safes? Sure, I know him.' He paused for a moment, thinking. 'He's not here, though. I haven't seen him round for a few days, actually.'

'Precisely,' I said. 'Do you remember the last time you saw him? I believe you gave him a note.'

'That's right!' said Oliver. 'I did. How did you know that?' Then he noticed Spencer standing a few steps behind me. 'She was there too, sir. She was there when I handed over the note. I remember now.'

'Okay, Mr Drong,' I said, 'I need you to tell me two things. Now, think carefully, and don't worry — whatever you say, you won't get into trouble. First, did you read what was in the note?'

Oliver looked shocked. 'No, sir!' he said indignantly. 'Of course not.'

'Not even a peek?' I said hopefully.

'Definitely not. It was a private note, sir. I would **never** read a private note.'

Curses! I thought. **Foiled by honesty!**

'Okay, Oliver,' I said. 'That's fine. But answer one more question. Can you remember anything about the rat who gave you the note?'

Oliver looked happy again. 'Oh, yes, sir. I remember that. I have a clear recollection of the rat who gave me the note. Remember it very well, in fact.'

Spencer came closer so she could hear better. **Now we're getting somewhere**, I thought.

'Right, Mr Drong,' I said briskly, taking out my notepad and pencil. 'Tell me everything. What did he look like?'

Oliver closed his eyes in order to concentrate better.

'Well,' he began, 'he was a rat.'

I waited.

Nothing.

'Yes?' I said. 'What else?'

'Um, well … he had fur. And whiskers. Fur and whiskers, that's right. He was pretty normal, really.'

'That's it?' I said.

'Pretty much,' said Oliver, opening his eyes. 'Fur and whiskers, I'm sure of it. **Oh! Oh!** I just remembered — he had a tail, too.'

I groaned.

'Mr Drong,' I said impatiently, 'you have just described every single rat in Rodent City. Surely there was something a little more distinctive about this particular rat? Think harder, please. Someone's life may depend on it.'

Oliver Drong thought harder. It was painful to watch — thinking was obviously something he spent very little time doing, and he wasn't used to it.

'There's one more thing,' he said, after quite a lot of eye-closing and brow-furrowing. 'He was fat.'

'Fat?' I repeated. **Fat?** That covers about **half** of all the rats in Rodent City.'

I should point out that rats are not, by nature, very healthy creatures. We eat too much and we don't exercise very often, so a fat rat is by no means an uncommon sight.

'This is getting us nowhere,' said Spencer. 'Let's get out of here.'

I decided to try one more time.

'Mr Drong,' I said. **Please** think hard. Is there anything else — **anything at all** — that you can remember about this particular rat who gave you the note? Anything **unusual**? Anything **different**?'

Oliver was looking more and more stupid by the second. He scrunched up his face again, as if thinking were something that caused him pain.

'**Weeeelll**,' he said, 'there was **one** more thing.'

'**What?**' said Spencer and I at the same time.

'He was carrying a bag.'

'A bag?' I said. 'What kind of bag?'

There was a long pause.

'Don't know,' said Oliver. 'Can't remember.'

Spencer and I turned to leave. Our only clue so far and it was a dead end.

What next? I wondered, as I trudged away from the counter.

I was halfway across the room when I heard Oliver's voice coming from behind me.

'Um, did I mention that he was completely white, with pink eyes? Like an albino?'

I froze. I looked at Spencer. Spencer looked at me. We both spoke at the same time.

'Kurt Remarque!'

'It wasn't a curt remark,' said Oliver, sounding hurt. 'I was only trying to help.'

'No, not a **curt remark**,' I said irritably. '**Kurt Remarque! Kurt Remarque!** The most famous rat in Rodent City. Or at least, he used to be. Don't tell me you've never heard of Kurt Remarque?'

Oliver looked at us both blankly. Young rats these days — they don't know **anything**.

'What do we do now?' said Spencer.

What indeed?

I suppose it is just possible that, like the foolish Oliver Drong, you've never heard of Kurt Remarque. The name may mean nothing to you, if you've been living under a rock with your eyes and ears closed and a bag over your head and another bag over that bag.

Well, all you need to know is this. One year ago, Kurt Remarque was the richest and meanest rat in all of Rodent City. Then he joined forces with a particularly bad bunch of monkey people, and cooked up an evil plot to poison all the rats in Rodent City and make an even bigger fortune.

Even though I am the greatest rat detective in the history of the world, I could never get enough evidence to prove that Kurt Remarque was evil and send him to gaol. After all, he had the Mayor and the old Chief of Police on his side as well. But with the help of the River Road Mouse Gang and a cranky old

caretaker called Boskin, I foiled his plot, sent him broke, and got rid of the Mayor and the Chief of Police at the same time.

Now **I** was the Chief of Police, Boskin was the Mayor, and Kurt Remarque was a poor, powerless rat **EEK**ing out a living by selling takeaway food from a little stall underneath the railway station. Or so I thought.

'There's only one thing we **can** do, Spencer,' I said. 'We have to go and see him.'

We took the Main Gutter Line, and headed for Snack Alley.

Right in the middle of town sits Central Station. Humans everywhere, rushing around, heading off to wherever it is that humans go. Who knows? Who cares? Cars, buses, taxis, shops selling hamburgers and newspapers and soft drinks.

Underneath Central Station are the platforms for the underground trains, rattling in and out along the tracks.

And underneath those platforms is Snack Alley. Have you ever been standing on a platform waiting for a train, looked down at the dusty, grimy tracks and seen a rat running along? Well, chances are that rat was heading for Snack Alley.

On this particular day, if you'd been on a particular platform at a particular time and happened to look down, you would have seen a rat **and** a mouse —

Spencer and me — running along the side of the tracks and disappearing down a grate. Someone obviously **did** see us — I heard a scream — but then we were gone.

Down the grate into a small drain, left at the first bend into an even smaller drain, and then through a hole in the drain into an air shaft below the platform. Snack Alley.

There were dozens of little stalls, each one selling something different. Popcorn, doughnuts, boiled sweets, crackers, hot dogs. Cheese too, of course, lots of cheese — but you'd be surprised how few rats really like cheese. Mice ran most of the cheese stalls; they love the stuff.

'Actually, I'm feeling a little peckish,' I said to Spencer as we pushed our way through the crowds of rodents that bustled up and down Snack Alley. 'There was a doughnut stall back there. I wonder if we might . . . ?'

'Certainly not!' said Spencer. 'How can you think of food at a time like this, Ocko?'

I can think of food at just about any time, but I didn't say that to Spencer. She may only be a mouse, but she can get surprisingly annoyed. I had enough on my hands without an aggravated mouse to deal with.

We trudged on, past Jake's Cakes, Trish's Fish Dish, Pop's Chop Shop and Fred's Bread Shed. My mouth was really watering by the time we got to Andy's Candy Stand.

'There it is!' I said.

28

KURT'S DESSERTS

I'd never bought anything there, of course. I wouldn't give Kurt Remarque a cent, no matter how wonderful his creamy, sweet desserts were.

It didn't look like anyone else would be buying his desserts today either. Kurt's dessert stand was closed.

'It's closed,' said Spencer.

'I can see that, Spencer. I'm the Chief

of Police. It's my job to notice things like that.'

The stand next door belonged to Jim. **Jim's Dim Sims** — a perfect snack to have before one of Kurt's desserts, or so they tell me.

I walked over. Jim was serving a family of rats.

'There we go, sir — a dozen mixed dim sims. Would you like soy sauce with that?'

'Yes, please,' said a middle-aged rat with three youngsters jumping up and down around him. 'Do you have any napkins?'

'Sorry,' said Jim. 'I'm all out.'

I felt sorry for the family — soy sauce can be very hard to get out of fur. But right now, I had other things to worry about.

'Excuse me,' I said. 'You must be Jim.'

'Wow, you must be a **genius**,' said Jim. 'How did you work **that** out?'

'Very funny, sir,' I replied. '**Most** witty. But I wonder if you could help me.'

'Only if you want dim sims,' said Jim.

'Actually,' said Spencer, stepping up beside me and smiling encouragingly at Jim, 'we are trying to find Kurt Remarque.'

'Never heard of him, miss,' said Jim. 'Care for a dim sim while we talk? Only fifty cents each — three for a dollar.'

'No, thank you, I'm not hungry,' said Spencer. 'You **must** know Kurt Remarque — he runs the dessert stand right next door to you.'

'Oh, **that** Kurt!' said Jim. 'Why didn't you say so? I stare at him every day, that sour-faced, fat, white-furred grump.'

'Yep, that's him,' said Spencer.

'So when did you see him last?' I asked.

Jim leant forward on the counter and began tugging thoughtfully at his whiskers.

'Now, let me see ... hmmm ... when did I see him last?' He looked at Spencer again. 'Are you sure you're not hungry, miss? It's just that I'm having a lot of trouble remembering, and you might as well have a bite to eat while you're waiting. Did I mention they're only three for a dollar?'

'The mouse is not hungry!' I said angrily. 'Now, just tell me when you saw him last!'

'Ah, well, you see; now I've forgotten altogether. Can't seem to remember at all.'

'This is **hopeless**,' I said to Spencer. 'Let's go.'

'Wait!' said Spencer. 'I have a brilliant idea!'

A brilliant idea? I thought. **A brilliant idea?** I'm the greatest police detective in Rodent City; **I'm** the one who has the brilliant ideas.

'Give me a dollar,' said Spencer.

'What for?' I asked.

'I'm feeling hungry all of a sudden. I think I might like — oh, I don't know ... three dim sims?'

'But you just said —' I began.

'I **know** what I said,' interrupted Spencer, 'but **now** I'm saying that I'm hungry.'

Mice!

I reached into my trouser pocket, handed over the coin, and Jim put three dim sims into a paper bag and passed them across the counter to Spencer.

'Soy sauce?' he asked.

'No, thanks,' said Spencer. 'So, how's your memory?'

'Suddenly it's amazingly clear,' said Jim with a grin. 'In fact, I can recall exactly when I last saw Kurt. It was ten days ago. Around lunchtime. Business was booming — lots of rats on their lunchbreaks — and I remember glancing over and seeing him serve one of his desserts to the ugliest rat I'd ever seen in my life.'

'An ugly rat?' said Spencer, as if she could hardly believe her ears.

'Hideous,' said Jim, 'and let's face it, I'm no oil painting myself. But this bloke looked like someone had inflated his head with a bicycle pump. Big teeth, too. Never seen anything like it. And this ugly rat was there for ages, eating his dessert and talking to Kurt for the longest time. I remember, because I was going to take a closer look, but I had to keep serving the customers. Like I say, it was a busy day. The next thing I know, I looked around and they were both gone.'

'Both of them?' I asked.

'That's what I said, pal. He must have just closed his dessert stand and walked off. Very strange. Hasn't been back since.'

Spencer and I looked at each other as we walked

away from the stall. I could tell we were both thinking the same thing.

Ten days ago. Just a couple of days before Patrick the Magnificent disappeared. This was no coincidence — this was a clue.

Our next step was obvious: we had to visit Kurt Remarque's home. We had to find out where he'd gone. But I didn't say this straight away — I had more important things on my mind.

'Are you going to eat those?' I asked Spencer.

'No way,' she replied, crinkling her snout. 'I **hate** dim sims.'

She handed over the bag, and I started eating. After all, it would be a shame to see them go to waste. They were surprisingly nice, but they would have been better with soy sauce.

****

Kurt Remarque lived behind a small green door set into a wall at the end of an alley, between two rubbish bins and a dumpster. Not the best-looking address, but behind that door is a very beautiful apartment. Believe me, I know — I've been there before. Most of the time, when you wind up knocking on Kurt Remarque's door, you know you're heading for some kind of trouble.

'Knock on the door,' I said to Spencer.

She knocked.

The door was answered by Kurt Remarque's ratservant, a tall, thin rodent in a long grey coat who looked down his nose at me.

'We're looking for Kurt,' said Spencer. 'Is he here?'

The tall thin rat said nothing for a few moments. Then he blinked. Then he sniffed. Then he spoke softly from the corner of his snout.

'Mr Remarque is gone,' he said.

'When will he be back?' I asked.

There was an even longer pause and another sniff before he replied. 'Never.'

'What do you mean **never**?' I asked.

'I mean exactly what I say,' said the ratservant. 'He will not be back. Ever. **Mr Remarque is DEAD.**'

CITY MOURNS AS LEADING RAT LAID TO REST

Large crowds are expected to line the streets of Rodent City today for the funeral of Kurt Remarque, former Mayor and one of the town's leading businessrats.

Mr Remarque died unexpectedly at his home yesterday, after a long and distinguished career serving the community and building a range of major businesses.

A spokesrat for Mr Remarque said he died from complications arising from excessive exercising.

'He was going for his daily run,' said the spokesrat, 'and he simply ran out of puff.'

Mr Remarque had recently led a quiet life, after losing much of his fortune in mysterious circumstances.

Before suffering that setback, however, he had donated to many worthy causes, and set a fine example for all young rats.

A service will be held at 3.00 pm at St Ratrick's Cathedral.

'Ha!' I said, throwing the paper to the floor.

I reached for my cup of tea and began to brood. Leading rat, indeed! Worthy causes! If only they knew.

'Well', said Spencer, 'what do you think?'

Spencer and I were having tea. Larry, Garry and Barry were there too. It was just like the old days: Ocko and the whole River Road Mouse Gang. Everyone except Patrick — he was still out there somewhere, missing.

'What do I think?' I said. 'I think it's bunkum. **Complete bunkum!**

'**Of course** it is,' chimed in Barry. 'He was nothing but a big fat crook. The only way he served the community was by robbing it.'

'I don't mean **that**,' I said. 'We all know he was a crook, but everyone else thought he was rich and important.' I picked up the paper again, and pointed at the story I'd just been reading. 'I mean all this stuff about how he died. Tell me, did you ever see Kurt Remarque run?'

'I never even saw him work up a sweat,' said Spencer. 'He was the fattest, laziest rat I ever saw.'

'Yeah,' said Larry. 'He was so rich and spoilt that he used to **hire** people to do his running around for him.'

'So what are you saying, Ocko?' said Spencer.

I leant back in my chair, like the super-smart investigative genius that I was, and fell over backwards.

I got up again, rubbing the back of my head and

trying to pretend that I meant
to fall over to get their attention. Lucky
rats have so much soft fur on the backs of their heads.

'What I'm saying,' I said carefully, 'is that I don't
believe for a moment that Kurt Remarque is dead.'

'Not dead?' said Garry.

'Not even sick,' I replied.

'So what's going on?' asked Spencer.

'I have no idea. But I do know one thing,' I said with
a flourish.

'What?' they all said at once.

'We're going to a funeral.'

****

St Ratrick's is a beautiful church — although you
probably know it as St Patrick's. A fine cathedral in the

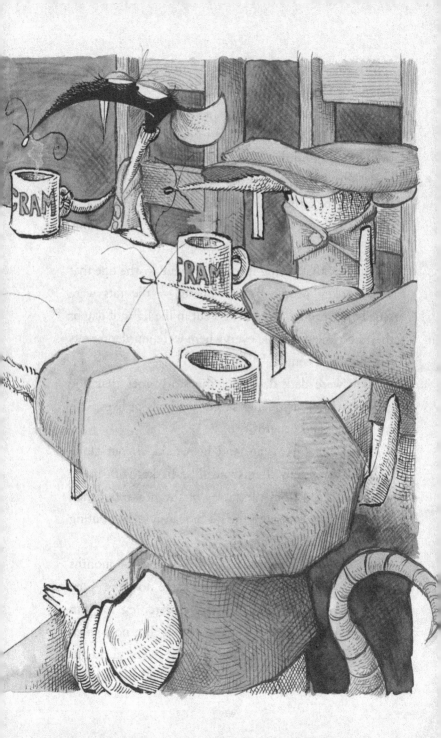

centre of town, with a tall Gothic spire and a magnificent white marble altar.

But underneath that altar is a crypt, and underneath that crypt is a drain that used to carry water. A lovely brick-lined drain that runs for hundreds of metres and leads into a huge cavernous room with candles lining the walls, beautiful wooden pews and a marble statue of a rat holding a basket right next to a simple stone altar. St Ratrick's.

They say that during the Great Plague — the one that you monkey people blamed on us — the rats were cruelly persecuted. Couldn't go out in the light of day or they'd be killed. People everywhere were murdering rats left, right and centre.

They were dark days, but the story goes that one brave rat single-handedly saved hundreds of lives with his courage and generosity.

Ratrick was his name, and he would go out alone into the dangerous streets and fill a basket with bread crusts gathered from the tables of the peasants. Then he would travel through the rat hideaways, distributing the bread for all to eat.

Ratrick kept whole communities going for months — until the terrible day when he came no more. One rat who ventured onto the streets searching for him came back with Ratrick's empty basket, but no sign of Ratrick himself was ever found. Did he die by accident, struck by a horse and cart? Was he killed by monkey people, or caught by a cat or dog? No one ever knew, but his legend lives on to this day.

Today, the cathedral that bears his name was all set up for a funeral. There were black crepe ribbons on the pews, a black cloth over the altar, and flowers, lots of flowers. But something was missing, thank goodness.

'Where's the coffin?' said Spencer.

'Not here, luckily for us,' I replied. 'The funeral is at three o'clock, which is still an hour away. So there's plenty of time.'

'Time for what?' said Spencer.

'You'll see,' I told her. 'Now, let's think. Barry, you're the strongest, so you'd better come with Spencer and me — I may need you. Larry and Garry, you two stay here and let me know if anyone comes into the church and heads our way.'

I led the way into a small room just off the altar,

where a ridiculously old rat was trying to pull a white robe over his head. It was caught around his ears, and he was staggering round and round in circles trying to finish the job. I went over and helped him.

'Thank you, my son,' he said, as soon as his snout was clear of the obstruction. 'These priestly robes can be quite awkward.' He patted the robe around his ample stomach then smoothed out his grey whiskers. 'Now, how can I help you? If you're here for the funeral, I'm afraid you're a little early.'

'Yes I know, Father,' I replied. 'But you see, I have a problem. I'm a very old friend of Mr Remarque —'

'**What?**' spluttered Spencer. 'You **hated** him, you — **OOMPFF!!**'

The **OOMPFF** was the sound Spencer made when I kicked her in the shins. Cruel, but effective.

'As I was saying, Father,' I went on smoothly, 'Kurt was a very dear old friend of mine, but I am afraid I'm leaving for the South Pole in fifteen minutes and I am not going to be able to come to the funeral.'

'The South Pole?' said the old rat. 'How **extraordinary**! Whatever are you doing **there**?'

'Er ... I'm an ice farmer,' I said, blurting out the first thing that came into my head. 'My friend Barry here carries the ice down to the dock one block at a time, and then we ship it back here.'

'Doesn't it melt on the way back?' said the old rat.

'Of course!' said Spencer quickly. 'Each block starts out the size of an elephant, but by the time the ship arrives, the blocks have melted to the size of ice cubes — perfect for putting in drinks.'

Spencer looked across at me as if I were an idiot, but I have to say it sounded like a very good cover story to me.

'Anyway,' I continued, picking up the story, 'my ship sails in a few minutes and there's no time to lose. I have to get to the South Pole before summer, or all the ice will melt.'

At this, the old rat in the priestly robe looked very suspicious.

'Surely the ice at the South Pole doesn't melt,' he said.

'Have you ever been there, Father?' said Spencer.

'No,' said the old rat slowly.

'Well, then, you'd be surprised,' said Spencer.

'Anyway,' I said again, before the old rat had time to ask any more questions, 'I am most desperately keen to pay my respects to dear Kurt, and as I can't be here for the funeral, I was hoping I could — that is, if you think it proper . . .'

The old rat looked at me expectantly. I was trying to think of a polite way to ask him where Kurt's earthly remains were. Spencer interrupted me, having thought of a way.

'Where's the body?' she said.

'Oh!' said the old rat, jumping as if he had received an electric shock. 'Oh! The body, of course . . . the body. You wish to pay your respects. Follow me.'

He led us out of the small room, past the altar, and out through another door. Barry waved at Garry and Larry, who were still sitting there in the empty church, looking bored.

We went down a set of steps and through another door into an even smaller room. It was empty except for a large trolley, and resting on the trolley was a large coffin.

'Dearly beloved,' said the old rat solemnly, 'here lie the mortal remains of our dear friend Kurt Remarque.' He pulled an old watch out of a pocket somewhere deep in his white robe and squinted at it. 'The pallbearers will be here in precisely fifteen minutes to carry it into the church, but until then you may have some quiet time to farewell your friend.'

And with that, the old rat turned and shuffled out, closing the door softly behind him. I waited until I heard his footsteps fade away as he ascended the stairs.

'Right,' I said. 'Barry, come over here and lift up the coffin.'

'Lift it up?' said Barry. 'Are you sure that's all right? It sounds a bit irreverent to me.'

'Nonsense,' I said. 'I'll bet you a dozen doughnuts that coffin is as light as a feather. If the body of Kurt Remarque is in there, I'll eat my hat.'

I had no intention of eating my hat, of course. It's a lovely grey fedora, perfect for a Chief of Police. But I knew I was right. After all, I am the brilliant Octavius O'Malley, the best rat detective in the world.

Barry walked over to the coffin, took a firm grip on one end, and lifted it — barely.

'UUGGH!' he said, and breathed out heavily. Then he put it down again.

'UUGGH?' I repeated. 'What do you mean **UUGGH**?'

'I'm sorry, Ocko,' said Barry, 'but that thing's heavy.'

'Heavy?' I said stupidly.

'Heavy,' said Barry. 'Heavy enough to hold the body of Kurt Remarque.'

'Looks like someone is having hat for dinner,' said Spencer, leaning lazily against a wall and gazing at her fingernails.

'Nonsense,' I said. 'Let me try that.'

I walked over to the coffin, grasped it firmly around one end, and lifted.

At least, I **tried** to lift it, but nothing happened. Heavy? It was **ridiculously** heavy. I took a firmer grip, heaved away, but still nothing. I was standing there, my arms wrapped around the coffin and my head pressed firmly to the top of it, struggling to lift it and feeling like a complete fool.

And that's when I heard it, as my ear was pressed to the side of the coffin and I was straining and grunting.

A noise. A tiny, faint noise like the sound of someone tapping or scratching.

I stepped back quickly, and stood staring at the coffin.

'There's something in there!' I said.

Spencer sighed, but didn't look up from her fingernails.

'Brilliant deduction, Ocko,' she said. 'We **know** there's something in there. It's the body of Kurt Remarque. He's fat, he's evil, he's dead, and he's in that box.'

'No, no,' I said hurriedly. 'There's something in there that's ... **alive**.'

That made Spencer look across sharply at me.

'What do you mean?' she said.

'I heard scratching ... or tapping,' I said. 'From inside the box. I tell you, **there's something in there**.'

'Okay, now you're freaking me out,' said Spencer.

'Barry,' I said. 'Quick, we only have a few minutes. Come over here and open this coffin.'

Barry is so strong he can lift a human with one hand, so he was the perfect mouse for the job. He took hold of one end of the coffin lid and pulled sharply on it. There was a piercing sound of splitting timber.

'**SSHHH!**' I hissed. 'We don't want that nosy old priest hearing you and coming back in.'

Barry pulled on the broken section of the lid a little more carefully, and gradually a piece the size of a large book began to come away.

I looked inside, and saw rocks. Lots and lots of rocks, each one the size of a tennis ball.

'**No wonder** it's so heavy,' said Spencer, who had been staring over my shoulder. 'But what was the noise?'

Just then, there was a sound of scrabbling and scratching from inside the coffin. We all jumped back. (We weren't scared, you understand, just cautious.)

As we watched, a small nose appeared. It sniffed the air, whiskers twitching, and then the nose climbed out of the coffin.

The nose was joined to a face, and some ears, and a body, and finally a tail.

'**PATRICK THE MAGNIFICENT!**' I said. '**It's you!**'

'It certainly is!' said Patrick. 'And I must say I'm extremely glad to see you. It was getting rather stuffy in there.'

Spencer ran over and hugged her little friend.

'Patrick, it's so good to see you!' she said. 'I was **so** worried. Where have you been? What happened? Were you kidnapped?'

'You bet!' said Patrick. 'And if you hadn't come along and found me, I would have been in some **real** trouble. What happened was —'

'Never mind about that now,' I interrupted. 'I hear footsteps. We've got to get out of here.'

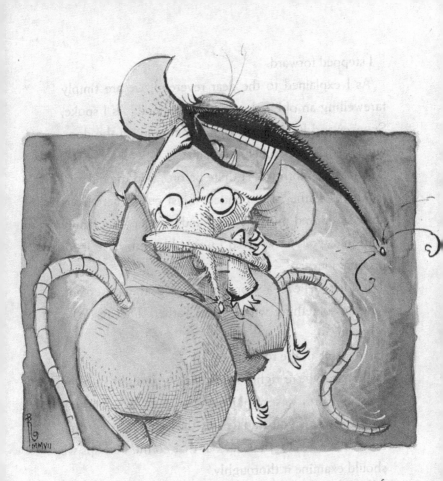

Barry quickly did his best to jam the broken piece of the coffin lid back in place. Spencer pulled a blue silk handkerchief out of her pocket and draped it across the broken corner, and just then the door burst open.

The old Reverend was back, but this time he was not alone. With him was Kurt's faithful ratservant, the long, thin miserable rat who had told us of his master's sad demise.

'What's going on?' demanded the ratservant.

I stepped forward.

'As I explained to the dear reverend, we are simply farewelling an old and much-loved friend.' As I spoke, Spencer and Barry were edging their way to the door, with Patrick hidden behind them.

'That blue cloth wasn't there before,' said the old rat.

'Ah yes, Father,' I responded. 'I just put it there. Kurt always admired my blue silk handkerchief — a family heirloom, you know — so I wanted him to have it for his final journey.'

'I don't believe a word of it,' said the ratservant. 'There's something wrong here, Father. They're up to no good.'

Everyone in the room froze.

'Perhaps you're right,' I said, staring straight into the eyes of Kurt's ratservant. 'Perhaps there **is** something wrong here. If you think that's the case, then we'd all better have a **very close look** at that coffin. Perhaps we should examine it thoroughly.'

The thin, gaunt rat stared at me with hatred gleaming in his eyes, and then, through pursed lips, he replied stiffly, 'No, on second thoughts, that probably won't be necessary.'

Barry, Spencer and the still-hidden Patrick were at the door by now, and so I strode over and hurriedly ushered them through.

'Well in that case, we'll be on our way,' I said quickly, and followed them through the door, hoping no one was paying enough attention to notice an extra pair of legs slipping through the door amidst the others.

I was in luck.

'Have fun at the South Pole!' said the old priest cheerfully as we left the room.

I just heard the voice of Kurt's ratservant muttering, 'The South Pole?' as we disappeared up into the church.

was having enough attention to notice
was hoping through the door and
It was in luck.
Have fun at the South Pole
cheerfully, as we left the room
I just heard the voice of Kate rejected as they
The South Pole as we headed off into the
chuch

5 PATRICK'S STORY

Half an hour later, Spencer, Patrick and I were safely back at Spencer's comfortable office at the Society for the Cooperation of Rats And Mice.

Larry, Barry and Garry had gone back to work — they had a load of food to deliver around Rodent City — so the three of us were settling down to a nice cup of tea and some well-deserved doughnuts. It was time to find out what had happened.

'Start at the beginning, Patrick the Magnificent,' I said, reaching for my third doughnut, 'and don't leave anything out.'

'Indeed I won't,' said Patrick, 'for it is a tale that will shake your very soul, a story of bravery and thrills, adventure and mystery, derring-do and surprise. You will be **amazed** at the stirring saga that is about to unfold before you. Never before in the history of Rodent City has one mouse had to endure such a series of **spectacular** and **spine-tingling** developments. Never —'

'Oh, for goodness' sake,' said Spencer, 'get to the point!

52

We're very happy to have you back safe and sound, Patrick, but if it takes you this long to tell us what happened, we'll be here forever. Just stick to the facts.'

'Okay, okay,' said Patrick. 'The facts. Now, let me see. I was about to open the main safe at the First Rodent Bank, using just a piece of chewing gum and a toothpick. Simple job, really, if you have the right tools and a brilliant mind ... Anyway, I was about to make the final adjustment, when one of the bankrats turned up with a note and distracted me.'

'Ah, yes,' I said through a mouthful of doughnut, 'that note. What was in it? It must have been very important to make you drop everything and race out the door.'

'It **was** important. More important than you could possibly imagine.'

Patrick reached into his waistcoat pocket, pulled out a single, crumpled sheet of paper and handed it to me. I flattened it out, held it up and read it out loud.

They've arrived, but there are only five left. Come quickly, and tell no one.

I looked across at Patrick, puzzled.

'**What's** arrived?' I asked.

'**Toothpicks**, of course,' said Patrick. 'Do you know how hard it is to get a good supply of toothpicks in this town? They are almost never available, and as soon as a box turns up they sell out really quickly. So I have a friend down at the markets who sends me a note as soon as some fresh supplies come in, then I race over and grab them before they all disappear.'

Spencer looked at me. I looked at Spencer. Neither of us could believe what we were hearing.

'Are you telling me,' I said, putting on my official Police Chief voice, 'that this all happened because you wanted to rush off and buy **toothpicks**?!'

'**Of course!**' said Patrick indignantly. 'What could be more important than that?'

'So how come you looked so scared when you read it?' demanded Spencer. 'I saw you — you looked terrified.'

'I certainly did,' said Patrick. 'Last time a batch came in, I waited half an hour before I went to get some, and I **missed out**!'

Mice! Sometimes they drive you mad, I swear.

'Okay, so what happened next?' I said. 'I presume the note was a fake?'

'I guess so,' said Patrick. 'I raced out of the bank and headed straight for Number Four Food Store, which is where my friend works. But when I got there, he said there were no toothpicks in stock, and he hadn't written me any note at all. I was pretty surprised, I can tell you, and suspicious too. So I raced out into the alley to get back to Spencer at the bank, and suddenly **WHAP!**

'**WHAP?**' said Spencer.

'Well, maybe it was more like **WHOMP!**,' said Patrick. 'Anyway, it was whatever sound a blanket makes when it's being thrown over your head so you can't see or hear anything. That's what happened to me, and the next thing I knew I was being bundled into some sort of barrow and wheeled through the streets.'

'Who was it? Who kidnapped you?' I asked.

It was a good question for a Chief of Police to ask, but it didn't do me much good.

'No idea,' said Patrick. 'No one said anything at all. They just wheeled me all the way across town, bumped me up a few steps, then pushed me into a small room. By the time I got the blanket off my head, the door was locked and I was alone.'

'**WOW!**' said Spencer. 'A real genuine kidnapping.'

'You bet!' said Patrick.

'Wait a minute,' I interrupted. 'You're Patrick the Magnificent. You can open any lock. Why didn't you just open the door and escape?'

Patrick looked a little embarrassed.

'Well,' he said, 'I can open any lock in the world, it's true, but not without my trusty chewing gum and toothpick. And you see, I rushed out of the bank in such a hurry that I left them behind.'

'You mean, without them you're helpless?'

'Pretty much, I'm afraid.'

'What is it you actually *do* with that chewing gum and toothpick, anyway?' I asked. 'I've always wanted to know.'

'Don't waste your time,' said Spencer. 'He won't tell you. It's his special secret. I've known Patrick for years, and I still have no idea.'

'Okay, so what happened next?' I said, to keep the story moving.

'Well, whoever it was who kidnapped me, they kept me there for **days and days and days**,' said Patrick. 'Every day, this rat I'd never seen before would open the door, toss in a bottle of water and a lump of cheese, then slam the door shut again. He wouldn't answer any questions — he never said a word — he just threw in the food and water, and then he was gone.'

'And that was it?' I asked.

'No way,' said Patrick. 'The best bit is still to come. Finally, after **days and days and days**, the door opened up and the rat came back in, but this time he was with someone else. And you'll never guess who it was!'

'Kurt Remarque,' I said.

Patrick just stared at me, his whiskers twitching in surprise.

'How did you know **that**?' he said.

'Simple,' I replied. 'That was his coffin we freed you from. Kurt Remarque is supposed to be dead and buried.'

'Well, he looked pretty healthy when he spoke to me,' said Patrick. 'Fit as a fiddle. Or to be more accurate, a double bass.'

'You bet,' said Spencer. 'There's something pretty fishy going on here, and I bet Kurt Remarque is behind it all — as usual.'

'So what did he say to you, Patrick?' I asked.

'Well, it was pretty weird, actually. He started out by being really friendly. "I'm awfully sorry," he said, "that you've been locked up in this horrid room. Most unfortunate. I'm making arrangements to have you freed immediately," he said. But then he added that before he let me go, there was just one thing he needed to know.'

'One thing?' I asked. I was on the edge of my seat by now. 'What was the one thing?'

'He wanted to know if I had seen any papers of his that he had left in the bank safe for security. "I know how good you are at opening things, Patrick the

Magnificent," he said, "so I presume you opened the bank safe. And if you opened it, then surely you couldn't resist peeking inside." I kept telling him I hadn't seen a thing, but he didn't believe me.'

'So what happened next?' said Spencer.

'Well, eventually he got up and left and the other rat came back with some fresh cheese and water. As soon as I ate it, I felt incredibly sleepy, and the next thing I knew I woke up inside some sort of stuffy box and started knocking, and it was broken open, and out I came — and there you both were!'

'So I guess they drugged you,' I said, getting up from my chair and walking across the room. I always think better when I'm moving. 'They drugged you and then tried to get rid of you, because they were worried that you knew too much.'

'Boy, it's lucky we turned up when we did,' said Spencer.

'Sure is,' said Patrick. 'But the funny thing is, I **don't** know too much. I don't know anything at all. I haven't seen **anything** in that safe. The note arrived before I even got a chance to open it.'

'Yes,' I said, rubbing my whiskers and pacing up and down, 'but Kurt Remarque couldn't afford to take that chance. There's something in that safe he doesn't want anyone to see.'

'Well then, we'd better go and take a look, hadn't we?' said Spencer.

'Exactly,' I replied. 'But how?'

'Easy!' said Patrick. 'You're the Police Chief, Ocko. You just march in there and tell them to open up.'

'I wish it were that easy, Patrick,' I said, 'but there are rules about these things. Safes are very private things, and you can't just go around opening them willy-nilly, even if you **are** the Chief of Police. Not unless you can prove that a crime has been committed, and we don't know anything about any crime.'

'So you can't open that safe?' said Patrick.

'Nope, but I know someone who can,' I said. 'You've got some spare chewing gum and toothpicks at home, haven't you, Patrick the Magnificent?'

We waited until dark before we returned to the First Rodent Bank. Spencer, Patrick and I slipped quietly down the side of the building — at least, we would have if it hadn't been for that large metal rubbish bin. Large and surprisingly hard to see. When I stubbed my big toe on it, it sounded like a gong ringing.

'SSHHH!' said Spencer crossly as I hopped about holding my left foot in both hands.

A rather pointless thing to say at that stage, if you ask me. After all, I wasn't **deliberately** yelling out **ouch, ouch, ouch, ouch** — I couldn't help myself. Anyway, it was nothing but sheer bad luck that as I hopped round and round in circles, my tail knocked the bin again.

This time it fell over with a loud crash, spilling old bottles, newspapers and tin cans across the alley. The lid went clattering down the alley, bounced off a brick wall and then settled slowly on the ground with that wonderful ringing echo that only a metal bin lid can make as it shudders to a halt.

'Ocko! For goodness' sake!' said Spencer. 'You might as well have brought a brass band with you. Perhaps we could sell tickets!'

'It's perfectly all right,' I replied crossly, trying to rub my toe and my tail at the same time, which sent me hopping in circles again. 'There's no one around at this time of night.'

'Let's hope not,' said Spencer, looking distinctly as if she didn't believe me.

Somehow we managed to find our way to the back door of the bank without any further incident. It was a stout, firmly locked door with the words **STRICTLY NO ENTRY** stencilled on it in white paint. Quite intimidating for anyone else, but no problem at all for Patrick the Magnificent.

'Okay, here's the plan,' I said. 'The fewer risks we take the better. So Patrick, I want you to break into the bank **and** into the safe. Spencer and I will wait out here. If anyone turns up, we'll knock loudly four times to warn you.'

'Sure,' said Patrick. 'Now, tell me again what I'm looking for when I open the safe.'

'I have no idea,' I replied. 'None whatsoever. All I know is that there's something in that safe that Kurt Remarque didn't want you to see. It was so important that he was prepared to kill you to keep his secret safe. We **must** find out what it is.'

'You bet,' said Patrick the Magnificent.

'But remember,' I added, 'you can't take anything out of the safe.' Leave everything exactly as you found it. Until we know what's going on here, we have to cover our tracks.'

'Righto,' said Patrick.

He strolled over to the door and stood there for a few seconds, staring at the lock. Then he cracked his knuckles. I winced; I **hate** that sound. Then he reached into his waistcoat pocket and pulled out a piece of chewing gum. He unwrapped it, popped it into his mouth and started chewing. He reached back into his pocket and this time came up with a toothpick. Then he took the chewing gum out of his mouth, leant down and began to fiddle with the lock.

I tried to see exactly what he was doing, but his fingers were too quick. He flicked the toothpick back and forth a few times, stretched out the chewing gum and pushed and pulled it, twisted his wrist and prodded and tweaked, and suddenly the door sprang open. With a flick of his tail and a hop and a step, Patrick the Magnificent was inside. The door swung shut behind him.

Spencer and I had nothing to do but wait. And talk ... but talking is something we haven't done too much of since our last big fight a few months ago. So we sat there and waited.

I rubbed my toe. Spencer picked at a clump of grass growing up between the cracks of the cobblestones. I rubbed my tail. Spencer whistled. Time passed.

****

Okay, I suppose you won't be happy until you know what the fight was about. Even though it was six months ago and it wasn't my fault at all.

I'll tell you, but first you have to remember one thing. I never liked mice much. Hated them, in fact. So it was a big thing for me to have a mouse as a friend.

After our last big adventure, Spencer and I had started the Society for the Cooperation of Rats And Mice. SCRAM, for short. You see, most rats were like me — they thought mice were a waste of space. Now that I knew better, I thought we could do something about it. So we did.

For the first few months, things went well. We organised a picnic, which was attended by dozens of rat and mouse families. They *did* tend to stick to their own groups a bit, but at least they didn't finish up playing the traditional rat games of 'Pin the Tail on the Mouse' or 'Mousehunt' or 'Chase the Mice with a Big Mallet and See How Many You Can Hit'.

After the picnic we had Rat and Mouse Information Day, where important rats and mice talked about their lives. Not so many rodents turned up to that, but the Combined Rat and Mouse Football Tournament and Sausage Sizzle a few weeks later was a huge success.

Then came the Society's first General Meeting, and as Police Chief I was the honoured keynote speaker. I spent three days carefully writing out my speech, and it was a great speech. Or so I thought.

I can still remember pretty much how it went.

Rodents one and all, thank you for coming today. It is, of course, an important day for all of us. But first, let me start with a joke. What do you say to a smart mouse? Nothing — smart mice don't exist! Wait, wait, here's another one. Did you hear about the mouse who tried to hold up a bank? It got too heavy, so he had to put it down! Get it? He had to put it down! And then there were these three mice who walked into a bar, and …

It was a great speech, but that was as far as I got before all the mice in the audience started throwing things at me. Me! The Police Chief and the most celebrated rat detective in all of Rodent City!

I went back to my seat, trying to dodge the rotten tomatoes being thrown at me (who brings rotten tomatoes to a meeting, anyway?). I sat back down beside Spencer and said to her, 'You never told me that mice have no sense of humour.'

Unfortunately, just at that moment, a very large and very rotten tomato came flying across the room and sailed straight into Spencer's face. **SPLAT!**

She jumped to her feet angrily and began wiping it away. 'Well, you never told me that you were still prejudiced against mice!' she replied, and walked straight off the stage.

Me? Prejudiced? There I was, just trying to make a few jokes, and that was all the thanks I got! Needless to say, I didn't go along to too many more SCRAM meetings after that. Imagine anyone thinking **I** was

form... meeting anyway, if I sat back down,
b... You... You've told me that
n...

prejudiced! I mean, **everyone** knows that mice aren't as
smart as rats. That's not prejudice; it's just a fact. And if
you can't make jokes about facts, what is the world
coming to?

So anyway, now you know. Our last fight was all
Spencer's fault. After that, she started blaming me for
not turning up to Society meetings any more. She said
I 'didn't care about improving relations between rats
and mice'. She said I was 'part of the problem, not part
of the solution'.

And now, half a year later, here we were — thrown

together by fate on another adventure, sitting in a dark alley waiting for a small mouse to come out of the back door of the First Rodent Bank.

****

And suddenly he did. The back door of the bank flew open and banged against the wall. Spencer nearly jumped out of her skin, but I was calm and cool. The only reason why I jumped three feet in the air was because I unexpectedly got a cramp in my foot.

'Pen and paper! Pen and paper!' said Patrick, who had raced out the door at a furious pace. **'Quick!** Does anyone have some paper? And a pen?'

'What's going on?' I asked. 'Did you find anything?'

'I found plenty,' said Patrick, 'but I have to write it down or I won't remember. I need pen and paper.'

'Here,' said Spencer, pulling a pencil and a small notebook from her pocket. 'Will this do?'

'Perfect,' said Patrick. He turned on his tail and disappeared back through the door, leaving Spencer and me staring blankly at each other.

'What was **that** all about?' asked Spencer.

'I have no idea,' I replied, 'but I guess we'll know soon enough.'

The two of us sat back down on the pavement and resumed our waiting.

After a minute or two, Spencer spoke.

'Ocko, what are we actually **doing**?'

'What do you mean?'

Spencer sat up a little straighter. 'Well,' she said, 'we found Patrick the Magnificent and he's safe now. Perhaps we should forget all this other nonsense and just go home.'

'We can't do that!' I said, trying to sound as shocked as I felt. 'We need to find out what Kurt Remarque is up to. Remember last time? He tried to poison the whole of Rodent City, and if we hadn't been there to stop him —'

'Yes, I know all that,' Spencer interrupted, 'but that's all in the past. If Kurt's done anything wrong this time, we should just refer it to the police. Officially, I mean.'

'It's too late for that,' I said. 'Haven't you forgotten that we never proved Kurt Remarque had done anything wrong last time either? We just foiled his evil plot and then sent all his money to charity. As far as the rest of the Police Force are concerned, he's just a businessrat who's fallen on hard times.'

'Yeah, **real** hard times, remember? The rest of Rodent City thinks he's dead!' said Spencer.

'Well, yes, there is that,' I admitted. 'But all the more reason for us to find out where he is and what he's up to — and we have to do that alone. That way, if he's broken the law, I can get my police officers to take over the case. But without any evidence, there's not much we can do.'

Just then, the door burst open and Patrick re-emerged.

'What have you got?' asked Spencer.

'I'm not sure,' he replied. 'But I know I've got **something**.'

'Well, let's not hang around here any longer,' I said. 'We're pushing our luck already. Let's go somewhere safe to talk.'

Spencer pushed the back door of the bank shut, and we scampered back up the alley and into the night.

'What have you got,' asked Spencer.

'I'm not sure,' he replied, 'but it's

something.'

'Well, let's not hang around here—'

'We're pushing our luck already if we

wait to talk.'

Spencer pushed the back door of the bank shut and

we scampered back up the alley and into the night

1
MONEY, MONEY, MONEY

Cecil's Night Owl Café is a great little establishment tucked away down a quiet laneway not far from my office. It serves good coffee and the best doughnuts in the city, and it's open all hours. You do see some strange rodents in there at times — a few menacing mice and the kind of rats you wouldn't want to corner in a dark alley — but everyone tends to mind their own business. I like it.

Spencer, Patrick and I were settled into a corner booth with a pot of coffee and a plate of Cecil's finest doughnuts.

'Okay, let's see what you've got, Patrick,' I said.

'Well, I got into the safe okay — that was no problem at all. Those Murgatroyd Splendid Supreme models are a piece of cake for me, especially the early 907b version. All it took was three pokes with the toothpick, and I —'

'Skip the details, Patrick,' said Spencer. 'We know you're the best safecracker in the business — you remind us often enough. What we want to know is what you found **inside** the safe once you got it open.'

'Well, money of course,' said Patrick, looking a little offended. 'Lots and lots of it — gold bars, banknotes and coins. But there were papers, too.'

'What sort of papers?' I asked.

'All sorts. Lots of documents about mortgages, bank accounts and loans, all filed away carefully in alphabetical order.'

'Did you look through them all?' asked Spencer.

'No way,' said Patrick. 'There wasn't enough time for that. I just went straight to **R** for **Remarque**, and this is what I found . . .'

Patrick reached into his waistcoat and, with a flourish, pulled out . . . a toothpick.

'Oh, sorry — wrong pocket,' he said. He reached back inside his waistcoat, rummaged around a bit more, and this time his hand emerged clutching a piece of paper, which he passed to me.

'Of course, that's just a copy,' he added hastily. 'That's why I needed the pen and paper. I left the original exactly the way I found it.'

'Good work, Patrick,' I said.

I carefully unfolded the slightly crumpled paper and set it on the table in front of me.

Spencer moved across to read over my shoulder.

STATEMENT OF ACCOUNT
Kurt Remarque

Date	Transaction	Amount	Total
19th Jan	Opening Balance	327.50	327.50
24th Jan	Deposit	200.00	527.50
30th Jan	Deposit	100.00	627.50

4th Feb	Deposit	50.00	677.50
11th Feb	Deposit	200.00	877.50
17th Feb	Deposit	100.00	977.50
23rd Feb	Deposit	250.00	1227.50
3rd Mar	Deposit	300.00	1527.50
9th Mar	Deposit	100.00	1627.50
14th Mar	Deposit	50.00	1677.50
20th Mar	Deposit	150.00	1827.50
26th Mar	Deposit	200.00	2027.50
30th Mar	Deposit	50.00	2077.50
31st Mar	Deposit	100.00	2177.50
1st Apr	Deposit	50.00	2227.50
2nd Apr	Deposit	50.00	2277.50
3rd Apr	Deposit	50.00	2327.50
4th Apr	Deposit	50.00	2377.50
4th Apr	ACCOUNT CLOSED		NIL

Funds transferred to Account 5909963
Banco Rata, Lima

'**Lima?**' said Spencer. 'What or where is **Lima**?'

'It's some sort of bean, I think,' said Patrick the Magnificent.

'You're right … and you're wrong, Patrick,' I said. 'Fortunately, as an extremely talented and experienced police chief, I put great store in keeping my general knowledge up to date. So I can tell you that the lima bean does indeed exist, and can be very tasty if you soak it in cold water for twenty-four hours and then cook it with onions, tomatoes and a little basil. But I believe you will find that the "Lima" mentioned in this document is, in fact, the capital city of Peru, in South America.'

'South America?' said Spencer.

'South America,' I repeated. 'Peru is approximately 1.28 million square kilometres, if I'm not very much mistaken. Bordered by Ecuador, Colombia, Brazil of course, Bolivia, and I think perhaps one other country, but I can't remember which. Sorry.'

'Very impressive,' said Spencer, her voice laced with something that sounded suspiciously like sarcasm. 'But why **Peru**? Why **South America**? What is this all about?'

This was obviously a case for a brilliant police mind like mine. I was in my element.

'Well, let's take a closer look,' I said. 'In January, Kurt had a little over three hundred dollars in his bank account. Not very much at all, really, for someone who used to have millions.'

'Yes, but hardly surprising,' put in Spencer. 'After all, we **did** take it upon ourselves to confiscate his ill-gotten gains a year ago.'

'So he started all over again, in a nice honest business,' I said. 'And look what's happened since then. Things must have been going well at the dessert stand. Check out all those deposits.'

Spencer looked over my shoulder again, and ran her finger down the long list of figures.

'Two hundred, one hundred, two hundred and fifty, three hundred . . . pretty impressive.'

'Yes,' I said. 'Almost three months of solid saving, and

then it all stops on the fourth of April.'

'Ten days ago,' said Spencer. 'What happened ten days ago?'

'Kurt disappeared,' I said, 'straight after he met that ugly, big-headed rat. And then just a couple of days later Patrick the Magnificent was kidnapped. And if you ask me, this piece of paper was exactly what Kurt Remarque didn't want us to see. He must have heard somehow that Patrick was testing the bank's security by breaking into the safe. It was obviously a risk he couldn't afford to take.'

'But what does it all mean?' said Patrick. 'Who cares about Lima and a couple of thousand dollars?'

'I don't know,' I said, folding up the paper and stuffing it into my coat pocket, 'but I mean to find out.'

I poured myself another cup of Cecil's fine coffee, took a bite of a plump jam doughnut, and watched in dismay as a squirt of bright red jam landed on my trousers.

I was still cleaning it off with a paper napkin when Spencer spoke up.

'Okay, Ocko,' she said. 'So tell me: what are we going to do, and why? You obviously have a plan in mind, so out with it. What next?'

I have to confess that I had no plan in mind at all. But when you've been a detective as long as I have, you develop a good nose for crime. And my very large snout was well and truly **itching** with suspicion right now. Something was going on, and it wasn't legal, I was sure of it. And at a time like this, a few minor details like not knowing what was going on and not having any sort of plan weren't about to stop me.

I finished wiping away the spilt jam, had a sip of coffee, and rubbed my itchy whiskers.

'Well, here's what I think,' I said carefully. 'Kurt Remarque saved up a nice little nest egg and secretly sent it to Peru. Then he kidnapped Patrick the Magnificent and tried to get rid of him to make sure no one found out. At the same time he faked his own death, and now no one knows where he really is. That could only mean one thing — Kurt Remarque has gone to Peru, and he's up to no good.'

'You think he's in Peru?' said Spencer.

'I'm sure of it,' I said, hoping it was true.

'So what now?'

'Well,' I said, getting up from the table and reaching for my coat, 'I think it's high time I took a bit of a holiday. I've been working too hard lately, and I think I need a trip to a nice warm country. Maybe somewhere in South America, somewhere like ...'

'**Peru?**' said Patrick.

'**Magnificent idea!**' I said. 'Anyone care to join me?'

8

THE CHASE BEGINS

It was all arranged. Deputy Smith was filling in as Chief of Police while I was on 'holiday'. Unfortunately, Larry, Garry and Barry were too busy with their food delivery business to join us on this new adventure.

'The orders are piling up', said Larry.

'Our customers need us,' said Garry. 'I've got four dozen cream buns that should have been delivered yesterday.'

I knew I'd miss their special skills, but I also knew that cream buns were extremely important, so I sent them off. Luckily, Spencer and Patrick were packed and ready to go.

I'd packed everything I needed for the trip in my small black travel case: two changes of clothes, a notebook, two pens, a toothbrush, a torch, a wallet filled with cash, two bottles of water, two packets of assorted doughnuts and four large packets of peanuts. It's not that I'm greedy, you understand — all that food is absolutely essential. After all, airline travel for rats and mice is a very basic affair. There's no in-flight service, that's for sure.

The departure lounge at the international airport is a wonderful place, full of bustling crowds wheeling trolleys full of luggage, well-stocked duty-free shops and very reasonably priced bars and cafés. Or so I've been told. Personally, I've never been anywhere near it. Let's face it, have you ever seen a mouse or a rat strolling through the glistening, well-polished halls of your local airport? Besides, security is way too tight for even the most talented rat to penetrate, with security guards everywhere and all the luggage X-rayed at least once. I suppose it would be possible for a rat of my talents to find a way in, but why would you bother? After all, just down the road from most big airport passenger terminals is a much better option for a rodent on the move. And that's exactly where Spencer, Patrick and I were headed this morning.

I took my travel case, locked my office behind me, and slipped down into the Sewer Walk for the quick trip across town to one of the big warehouses. Spencer and Patrick were waiting for me there. Spencer had a small blue backpack slung over her shoulder, and Patrick had — **what on earth??** — Patrick had a **massive suitcase** on wheels that was taller, wider and thicker than the three of us put together. There was another smaller red bag as well, strapped to the top of it.

'What have you brought with you?' I asked.

'Just the essentials,' said Patrick.

I sighed. 'Okay, open it up.'

'I assure you, everything in there is **absolutely essential**,' protested Patrick, unzipping the massive case and hauling open the lid.

I looked inside. There were jumpers and coats and an umbrella and four pairs of boots and the entire works of Shakespeare in four leather-bound volumes and a picnic set and an iron and a kettle and three tennis balls and a tennis racket and a pocketknife and some pyjamas and a dressing gown and a writing case filled with pens and pencils and crayons and two jigsaw puzzles and a pith helmet and a hammer and a set of screwdrivers and a stack of comics and a large portable radio and ...

'What's in the small red bag?' I asked.

'Oh, just a couple of changes of clothing and some toiletries for the trip,' said Patrick.

I reached into the large case, removed the pocketknife and handed it to Patrick.

'As it happens, I've forgotten my trusty pocketknife, so put this in the red bag. But the suitcase and everything else in it stays here.'

'But that's **impossible**!' protested the little mouse. 'I can't **possibly** survive without my basic supplies. And what if we come across a tennis court?'

'We **won't** come across a tennis court,' I said. 'And as for Shakespeare, he can stay at home and wait till you come back.'

'But I read Shakespeare **every day**!' wailed Patrick.

'Trust me,' I said. 'I must be cruel, but only to be kind.'

'But I'll be like a mouse without a tail!' he said.

'Whatever,' I replied wittily.

We found a spot behind two huge oil drums in the corner of the warehouse to hide Patrick's enormous suitcase. Then we started looking around for an airport truck. That didn't take long. Every morning, dozens of huge trucks left the warehouse with all sorts of goods destined for overseas. Some were in huge metal containers carried on the back of very large trucks; some were smaller boxes and satchels in little vans.

Sure enough, there were a couple of these smaller vans loading up already. We waited until the driver stopped for a quick cup of coffee, and then slipped inside. Soon we were comfortably settled in a corner between two sacks of mail. The driver shut the doors, hopped in, and took us through town, down the highway, straight past the international passenger terminal and into the cargo-loading warehouse. Perfect!

The trick is getting out of the van without being noticed. You can't just charge out as soon as the door is opened, but you can't wait inside forever either, because sooner or later the humans will unload the last of the boxes and find you sitting there looking like an idiot. Then they'll scream or yell and soon everyone will be running around with sticks and brooms trying to kill you. Monkey people, most of them, are stupid **and** violent.

So we waited, but we didn't wait forever. Spencer peeked out from behind the sack and watched for the moment when the man unloading the van paused (just for a few seconds) to scratch his nose or pick up something he dropped or chat to the other driver.

'**Now!**' she hissed, and the three of us nipped out the door of the van, scuttled past a row of boxes on the floor and disappeared into the warehouse.

What you may not know is that all those big boxes and containers that get loaded onto cargo flights around the world are not X-rayed or checked as closely as the luggage that goes onto passenger flights. So that makes cargo planes the preferred mode of transport for rats around the world. All we needed to do now was stroll up and down the aisles of the warehouse and find the right label.

NEW YORK ... **LONDON** ... **ROME** ... **SHANGHAI** ... **DUBAI** ... **HONG KONG** ...

'This is going to be difficult,' said Spencer as we wandered up and down. 'What gets sent to Lima, anyway?'

'I guess they don't need any lima beans,' said Patrick. 'What **do** they need?'

I rubbed my whiskers thoughtfully and tried to remember everything I could about Peru. Dry desert plains in the west, the Amazon jungle in the east, and the rugged Andes mountains in the middle. Hmmm, mountains ...

'That's it!' I said. 'Mining equipment! They have mountains in Peru, and that means they have gold mines and copper mines and silver mines. And if they have mines, then they need heavy equipment to mine it. **Follow me.'**

I led the way to the back of the warehouse, where the big machinery was usually stored. Sure enough, there were tractors and engine parts and huge wooden crates full of tools and strange metal contraptions.

'Spread out,' said Spencer. 'Check the labels.'

We each chose an aisle and moved down it quickly.

KARRATHA ... ODESSA ... UKRAINE ... POLAND ... MOUNT ISA ... ARKANSAS ... NEWCASTLE ...

'Brazil!' whispered Patrick from his aisle. 'I found Brazil. Isn't that near Peru?'

Spencer and I raced over to join him. There were three big boxes and a tractor all labelled **DESTINATION: BRAZIL**.

'Keep looking,' I said. 'I think we're on the right track.'

BRAZIL ... BRAZIL ... BRAZIL ... ARGENTINA ... CHILE ... ECUADOR ... PERU!

'Bingo!' I yelled.

'SSHH!' said Spencer.

'Where's Bingo?' said Patrick. 'Is that somewhere near Peru?'

'Bingo is an expression of discovery, Patrick,' I said. 'This crate is going to take us all the way to Peru, non-stop!'

All three of us stared at the sturdy wooden crate that

would be our home for the next couple of days. I was a little concerned at the word **DANGER** written on the outside in several places, but beggars can't be choosers, as they say.

'Where's that pocket-knife of yours, Patrick?' I asked.

'Unlike my tennis racket, my Shakespeare and my jigsaws, it's right here,' said Patrick grumpily. 'Pity we don't have a hammer too, isn't it?'

'Well, we'll just have to survive,' I said.

'See if you can prise open a corner of this crate, but do it **very** carefully.' I was still thinking about those **DANGER** signs.

Patrick set to work with his knife while Spencer and I kept a lookout. Within a few minutes he had lifted one of the boards just far enough for the three of us to slip inside with our bags.

'Okay, find a spot and get comfortable,' I said. 'This will be our home until we hit Peru, and goodness knows how long **that** will take.'

The crate seemed to be filled with smaller boxes, but there was enough room for us to find a spot to stretch out.

'Pretty good going,' I thought to myself. **'Watch out, Kurt Remarque, we're on your tail!'**

I fished out my torch and flicked it on quickly to see what was in these so-called 'dangerous boxes'.

Printed on the side of each box was the word **GELIGNITE**.

Explosives. What fun.

Flying through the air inside a box of explosives is not necessarily the most relaxing and comfortable way to travel. Needless to say, we didn't sleep a lot.

The cargo plane was pretty bumpy, and every time things got rough, the others got worried. **I** was calm and relaxed, of course, being a very experienced and brave police detective, but Spencer and Patrick were nervous wrecks.

'Watch out!' I squealed, as the plane rocked back and forth through the clouds. 'I think that top box of gelignite is about to fall!'

'Relax, Ocko,' said Spencer for the four-hundred-and-thirty-seventh time. 'I'll say it again: gelignite won't explode just because it falls over. Probably not, anyway.'

'Probably not? **Probably** not?' I yelled. 'What do you mean **probably**? Does that mean there is a small chance it **will** explode?'

'It means there is a small chance I will **kill** you if you don't sit down and relax!'

'I don't know about Ocko, but I could relax a bit more if I had my Shakespeare to read,' moaned Patrick.

And so it went on, hour after hour, bump after bump, as we soared through the skies heading for South America.

After a while we ate a few of my doughnuts, drank a little water and tried to sleep. It was a **long** flight.

Eventually, the droning engines of the cargo plane started to make a slightly different, lower noise. Patrick the Magnificent sat up and sniffed the air.

'We're going down,' he said matter-of-factly.

'Going down?' I yelled, clutching at Spencer's arm. '**Going down?** We're **doomed!** We're **going to crash!**'

'**No**, Ocko,' said Spencer calmly. 'He means we've started our descent. We're going to **land**.'

'I knew that,' I lied. 'I was just making sure.'

I **hate** flying.

We couldn't see anything out of the windows of the plane, for two very good reasons. First, cargo planes don't have windows, except for the one the pilot looks out of. And second, we were inside a wooden crate full of explosives.

But after a while the plane began to bank and turn, flying in a slow circle. My ears popped, there were a lot of mechanical whirrs and bumps and grinding noises, and then a loud *THUD*, and we were on the ground.

It was at least another hour before we heard the sound of the plane's cargo doors opening. There was a very small gap in the crate where Patrick had forced it open, and as I peeked through I could see forklift trucks starting to unload the crates.

'**Oi!** Watch out for this lot. They're highly explosive,' came a voice from outside. Then there was a jolt and a scrape and we found ourselves being lifted through the air and carried off to where a line of trucks waited.

As our box was swung onto the back of an open-tray truck I looked out through the gap again, and glimpsed a sign saying **LIMA**. 'Good,' I thought, 'at least we were on the right plane.'

I suppose you're wondering what a rat does when he hits a new city. Is there a Rodent Information Bureau? A Travelling Rat Society? Well, not quite. Of course, there are rats in every major city of the world, but you have to work out for yourself how to find them. We don't exactly advertise ourselves and we don't always welcome strangers.

At first glance (seen through the wooden planks of a box), Lima looked like every other city in the world: big, loud and crowded. The main difference seemed to be that the roads were very bumpy, which is not a good thing when you're on the back of an open truck leaning on a stick of gelignite.

Spencer must have been thinking exactly the same thing.

'How do we get off?' she said. 'What's the plan?'

'What is your **obsession** with **plans**?' I said. 'How many plans does one rat need?'

'**Just one** would be a good start,' replied Spencer. 'And anyway, I'm a **mouse**.'

'Okay, **here's** a plan,' I said. 'Let's just get out of here. Everyone, grab your bags.'

It only took a few seconds for Patrick to lever open the side of the box once more, and soon the three of us were standing on the edge of the truck, staring at the road rushing past below us. We were travelling so fast that the wind was pushing my whiskers back against my ears, and my ears were flapping like flags.

I waited until the truck slowed a little to turn a corner, then I yelled, '**Jump!**'

No one moved an inch. Patrick stood there clutching the side of the truck. Spencer stood there clutching Patrick. I stood there wondering why no one had moved.

'I said, **"Jump!"**' I repeated.

'Jump where?' said Spencer. 'To our certain deaths?'

'Looks positively dangerous to me,' said Patrick.

Mice. Typical.

Just at that moment, the truck bounced over a particularly large pothole and veered sharply to the right. The three of us were thrown, bags and all, into the air, and suddenly there was no truck underneath us any more. We tumbled onto the road, and I felt myself rolling head over heels, luckily still clutching my bag. I caught a quick glimpse of Spencer before she disappeared headfirst down a drain, then the next thing I saw was the wall of a building heading straight for me.

SPLAT! I finished up with my feet in the air, my head on the pavement, and my tail wrapped around my body in a **most** uncomfortable fashion.

'**That** worked well,' said a small red bag on the footpath nearby. The bag wobbled, then shifted sideways, and Patrick the Magnificent crawled out from under it. 'Luckily the ground broke my fall,' he said, rubbing his tail. He looked around. 'Where's Spencer?'

'Down there,' I said, pointing to the drain. I disentangled myself from my own tail and staggered to my feet. 'We'd better go down and find her.'

We made our way over to the gutter and peered into the drain.

'**Spencer?**' I called. '**Are you down there?**'

'Come on down,' Spencer's voice came echoing back. 'I've found a path.'

****

Most drains in most cities are pathways for rats, mice and other small animals going about their daily business. Lima was no exception. Patrick and I collected our bags and slipped down into the drain. Spencer was sitting on her backpack at the bottom, rubbing the side of her face, which had a long pink scratch down it.

'Are you okay?' I asked.

'I'll live,' said Spencer, getting to her feet. 'But check this out,' she added, pointing away to her right.

I looked in the direction of her finger, and sure enough, there was a long pathway heading off into the shadows. You could tell that animals used it, because on the wall someone had scratched a crude arrow and the words Centro de la Ciudad.

'What language is that?' said Patrick. 'It must be Peruvian.'

'I don't know,' said Spencer. 'It looks like Spanish to me. In Spanish, that would mean something like **This way to the centre of town**.'

'Sure, but we're **thousands of miles** from Spain, aren't we?' said Patrick. 'They would hardly speak Spanish way over here, would they?'

'**Of course** they do,' I said, displaying my superb general knowledge once again. 'The Spanish invaded and conquered Peru hundreds of years ago, and they've been speaking the language here ever since. Now, that's it for today's history lesson — let's keep moving.'

We started walking down the narrow pathway, which was lit every few metres by sunlight filtering through the stormwater drains.

Every now and then we would hear music drifting down from the streets above. Sometimes we would hear shouts, or car horns, or yelling, or the sounds of cars and trucks driving above us. Lima sounded like a busy city.

It wasn't long before small groups of rats and the

CENTRO DE LA
CIUDAD →

occasional mouse began to pass us on the pathway. I tried to talk to one or two of them to ask directions, but they mostly ignored me or answered in a language I couldn't understand. Sometimes they stared at us, or pointed at our strange clothing, but mainly they just walked past us quickly without talking at all. The local rats all seemed to wear a kind of multicoloured blanket with a hole in it to stick your head through. Ponchos, I think they're called.

The noise above us got louder and louder, until eventually it sounded like we were walking beneath a huge party.

'Let's go up and check it out,' said Patrick, and so, of course, we did.

It was the biggest market I'd ever seen in my life. It easily took up a whole city block, with row after row of little wooden stalls selling food, animals, rugs, pots, pans — everything you could possibly imagine.

There were people everywhere, most of them carrying wicker baskets or cloth bags full of the things they had bought. They wore ponchos just like the rats.

Spencer, Patrick and I stood quietly behind the wooden leg of one of the tables and watched the crowds go by.

Spencer pointed to the stall directly opposite us. 'Look at all that,' she said wistfully.

The table was laden with piles of bananas, beans, ears of corn, chilli peppers and huge glistening melons. Next to it was another stall selling freshly baked bread, still steaming from the oven. I looked carefully, but there were no doughnuts.

'Are you hungry, my friends?'

The voice came from behind us. I turned around.

Leaning against the wall was a very short, very fat rat with dark, drooping whiskers. He was wearing a red, green and yellow poncho and picking lazily at his teeth with a toothpick. As we all stared, he spoke again.

'You speak English — no? English?'

'Yes,' said Spencer, surprised. 'How did you know?'

The fat rat laughed and tossed the toothpick onto the ground. I looked over at Patrick and I could tell he was dying to pick it up and add it to his collection.

'Well,' said the stranger, still chuckling, 'you don't look like locals. In fact, you look a little lost.' He waddled over to us and stuck out his hand. 'José is the name — José Manuel Carlos Maria Pedro de Ollantaytambo. Welcome to Peru.'

'Octavius O'Malley,' I said, shaking his hand. 'And these are my friends, Spencer and Patrick. And you are indeed correct — we are visitors here. In fact, we've just arrived.'

'Then you must be hungry,' said José.

'Follow me.'

José scuttled off down the path, dodging the legs of passers-by. We followed, darting in and out and trying to keep up with his swirling poncho as it disappeared around corners and moved neatly in and out of the crowds.

After a while, José slipped between two big rubbish bins, and we followed. We came out into a long, narrow alley that ran behind a row of food stalls. There were boxes and boxes of fruit, vegetables and all sorts of other foods stacked up ready for sale.

'Welcome to Café José,' said José, waving at the boxes. 'It is self-service, my friends, but I advise you to be quick. If the stallholders spot you, they will chase you. And believe me, you don't want to be caught.'

Spencer, Patrick and I spread out and moved quickly down the alley, filling our pockets with food as we went. Things went well until the very last stall, where Patrick the Magnificent spent just a **little** too long selecting precisely the right size of cashew nut from a box.

'Al diablo con esos malditos ratones!'

It was the shrill voice of an old woman, who suddenly emerged from one of the stalls waving an enormous straw broom. She ran straight at the box of cashews, swiping at it with the broom.

She was quick, but fortunately Patrick was quicker. He dodged the flailing broom, darted across the alley and ran back into the shadows near the bins, where the rest of us were waiting.

'Bravo!' said José, laughing. 'You run fast, little mouse! Now come, sit and eat with me.'

He led us through a small opening in the wall at the end of the alley, down a few steps, then through an even smaller hole, and we found ourselves in a large, airy storeroom.

'No one will disturb us here,' said José as he lay back on a pile of hessian sacks. 'These are my private living quarters. Make yourselves at home.'

We spread out the food we had managed to gather. Nuts, cherries, a hunk of cheese, a circle of bread, some tomatoes (a little squashed) and a large dark green avocado. It was a real feast, and the four of us began demolishing it straight away. There is nothing like a long plane trip followed by a life-and-death broom chase for working up an appetite.

'So tell me,' said our host between mouthfuls of bread and cheese, 'what brings you to Lima? It is most unusual to see rats and mice travelling together. This would **never** happen in **my** country.'

'Nor in **our** country,' said Spencer, looking in my direction. 'I guess you could say circumstances have thrown us together.'

'We're searching for a ... for a ... a friend,' I added, choosing my words carefully. 'We have reason to believe he is somewhere in Lima.'

'Ah, well, Lima is a very big town,' said José, leaning back on the hessian sacks and scratching his huge stomach thoughtfully. 'So tell me, why has this friend of yours come to Peru?'

'We don't know,' I confessed. 'It's a bit of a mystery, really.'

'A **mystery**?' said José. 'Well, this is a town full of mystery, my friends. People come to Lima for many reasons. Some are here to build a new future for themselves, others just want to hide from their past. There are rats who come to make their fortunes, and rats who just come to make trouble. I wonder which kind your friend will prove to be.'

'A bit of both, I suspect,' said Spencer. 'Our friend has been known to cause trouble before. We want to make sure he doesn't cause any trouble here in Lima.'

'Hmm, most interesting,' said José. 'It is, as you say, a mystery. Well, why don't you tell José what you know about this friend, and I will help you find him.'

I looked carefully at our new friend, José Manuel Carlos Maria Pedro de Ollantaytambo (I have a good memory for names). He was being **very** helpful — almost **too** helpful. A good rat detective (and I am the best) learns to be very suspicious of other rodents, and José was making me suspicious. **Why** was he being so helpful? What was he after? Could we trust him? I certainly wasn't going to tell him who our 'friend' really was — not just yet, anyway. But without someone to help us, it was going to be very tricky tracking down Kurt Remarque in this strange new city. **Tread carefully, OcKo,** I thought to myself.

'Oh, we couldn't possibly impose on you, José,' I said. 'You've done enough for us already. I'm sure we'll find our friend somehow.'

José smiled a little, and scratched his stomach again.

'Ah,' he said. 'I see you do not trust me.'

Of course we do,' said Spencer quickly. 'It's just that —'

'No, no, it is fine,' said José. 'I understand.'

He leant forward, stroked his long, drooping whiskers, then fixed us with his large, brown eyes.

'Let me tell you a story, my friends,' he began. 'When I was a little rat, not much bigger than your mouse friend here' — he pointed at Patrick, who was settled in a corner chewing on a cherry — 'I lived with my parents in a tiny village in the valley of the ancient Incas. It was a beautiful place, my friends. We were very poor, but life was good. There was sunshine, water, a little food, and what rat needs more than this?

'But one day some humans came to the place where my family lived. They were strangers from far away, who spoke a language I did not understand. They had come to take things from the village, all sorts of things, which they carried away in a big truck.

'When they came to the building where we lived, my parents were worried. They hid me inside a vase.

How could they know what would happen? These strangers, they took the vase with them.'

'What happened?' said Patrick.

'Well, the truck drove away with all the valuable things from the village inside it.'

'The vase too?' said Patrick.

'Yes, my little friend,' said José, 'the vase ... and me inside it. I never saw my beloved parents again.'

'Never?' said Patrick, his eyes wide. 'That's **terrible**.'

'It was **indeed** terrible,' said José, and he wiped a tear from one eye. 'But you will be surprised when I tell you that I was a lucky rat that day, a very lucky rat. For even though I lost my family and my home, my life was saved, and I lived to tell the tale of my great adventure.'

'What happened?' said Patrick again.

'Well,' said José, 'that truck travelled for four days. The back was locked the whole time. When it finally stopped, I was weak with hunger and thirst, but I managed to crawl out of the vase and escape while they were unloading.'

'So you were safe?' said Spencer.

'Not yet, my friend, not yet. I was in a strange country where people spoke a strange language and I knew no one.'

'So how can you say you were lucky?' I asked.

'Because I met a fine rat that day,' said José, his eyes smiling. 'His name was Roy, and he was like a second

father to me. He could see that I was scared and half dead, and he took me home to his family. He fed me and cared for me, and as the days turned into weeks and then months, he taught me to speak the strange language that you call English.'

'How did you get back here, to Peru?' I asked.

'Ah,' said José smiling, 'Roy was a very clever rat. He had many big books in his home, and when I told him about the valley of the Incas, he found a book and showed me a map of where my home was. Together we planned the journey I would take and the roads I would use. It took a long time, many weeks, but I made my way back home to my village.'

'But you said you never saw your parents again,' said Spencer. 'Why not?'

'When I returned to the village, many months had passed and my parents were gone. I never found out where, or why. The village was even poorer than before, and there was almost no food. So like many other rats, I came here to Lima. Things are good here and I have made a good life. So you see, I was saved by the kindness of a stranger, and ever since then I have always helped travellers I meet along the way.'

It was a long story, and when he finished José leant back on the hessian sacks again and took another bite of bread and cheese.

I looked at Spencer and Patrick and I knew they

were both thinking the same thing as I was. This was a rat you could trust.

'The rat we are looking for in Peru is not really our friend, José,' I began. 'He is an evil rat, who makes trouble wherever he goes. He nearly destroyed our town once, and I am worried that he has come here to cause more trouble. We have to stop him.'

José's eyes lit up. 'Ah, this is a big adventure, my friends. A very big adventure. Who is this evil rat of whom you speak?'

'His name is Kurt Remarque,' I said. 'He has white fur and pink eyes, and he is very fat.'

'Fatter than I am?' said José, his stomach wobbling with laughter.

'Yes, even fatter than you,' I said, hoping that didn't sound rude.

'Well, I certainly haven't seen him around here, then,' said José. 'I would remember such a rat. But how do you know he has come to Peru?'

'Ah, that's easy,' said Spencer. 'He transferred all his money to a bank in Lima.'

'Ah, yes, I see,' said José. 'We have a saying here in Peru: **If you want to catch a mouse, go to where the cheese is.**' He looked across at Patrick and Spencer. 'No offence, my little friends. But it means that if you want to find this Kurt, you must follow the money.'

'My thoughts exactly,' I said. 'So we need to find the Banco Rata. Can you help us?'

'But of course!' said José. 'It will be our adventure. But I must warn you, while finding the bank will be easy, the rest will be difficult.'

'Difficult? Why?' I asked.

'Ah, you will see, my friends,' said José. 'You will see.'

'Okay, José, leave it to me,' I said in my best official police voice. Of course, José had no idea that I was a leading police detective back home in Rodent City, but I'm sure he found my voice impressive anyway. **Everybody** does.

We were standing outside the main city branch of the Banco Rata, which had an impressive brick entrance in a basement just below the Banco de Credito, which is the bank the monkey people use. It wasn't a long way from the market, but it had taken a while to get here because José had led us through all the narrow back alleys to avoid notice. Now it was time for me to do my stuff.

'But my friend,' said José, 'it will be difficult. You cannot just walk in and ask about one of their clients. You must have a **plan**.'

Everybody wants a **plan!** What is this **obsession** with **plans?**

'My plan,' I said to José, 'is to walk in there and ask

about Kurt Remarque, and I expect them to tell me what I need to know. Just watch and learn, José. If you know how to handle yourself, the rest is easy.'

José, Spencer and Patrick stood in the doorway and watched as I marched up to the counter of the bank. Almost straight away an elderly, stooped bankrat leapt up from his desk behind the counter and strode with remarkable speed in my direction. **This is more like it,** I thought.

'Le puedo ayudar, Señor,' he said, bowing slightly to me.

'Do you speak English?' I said.

'But of course,' said the old rat, 'anything to be of assistance. Now, if Señor could just tell me his account number ...' he added, producing a heavy gold pen from his inside pocket.

'Well, I don't have an account here, but ...' I began.

The old rat froze with the pen still in mid-air. He fixed me with a suspicious frown.

'Has Señor come here to *open* an account?'

'Well no,' I went on quickly, 'but I am hoping you can help me —'

Before I could finish my sentence, there was a shrill, ear-piercing whistle. It took me a moment to realise that it was coming from the old bankrat. It was so loud it sounded like a kettle boiling.

'I simply want some information!' I yelled, trying to make myself heard over the whistle.

The old rat stopped whistling. The bank became hushed and quiet, but my ears were still ringing.

The old rat's whiskers twitched slightly, and he stared at me as if I were some sort of monster. He was clearly horrified.

'**Information?**' he shrieked. '**Information?** You want ... *information?*'

He took a deep breath, and lifted the bony fingers of one hand, placing them to his lips. The whistling began again, and if possible it was even louder than before.

Two huge rats dressed in black suits rushed at me, one from my left and one from my right. They each grabbed one of my arms. I felt myself being lifted on to my tiptoes and marched down the bank chamber towards the door.

'Wait! Wait!' I spluttered. 'There must be some mistake! I only wanted — *OOOMPPHH!*'

On this particular occasion, the *OOOMPPHH!* was the sound I made as I landed on the dusty ground after the two goons had tossed me out of the bank.

I got up, dusted off my trousers and looked around. Spencer and Patrick were staring at me open-mouthed. José was leaning on the wall, chewing casually on a piece of celery.

'I tried to tell you, my friend, it is not so easy here in Peru,' he said.

'But all I wanted was **information**,' I said indignantly. 'I didn't even get to ask them a single question.'

'Ah yes,' said José, tossing away the last of the celery and coming over to me, 'but you must understand, my friend. Information is a very important thing here in Lima.'

'What do you mean?' I said.

José put his arm around my shoulders, and began to lead me away from the bank entrance. He spoke to me in a low, quiet voice.

'There are many things happening in a town like Lima. Some of them are legal and very normal, like running a business, selling a few things ... owning a shop. All very nice, all very legal. But other things, well, other things are perhaps not so legal. In Lima you can get rich very quickly if you are a smart rat who doesn't mind bending the rules.'

'But that's true everywhere,' I said. 'We have crooked, dirty rats at home as well. Kurt Remarque used to be one of them.'

'Yes, of course,' said José. 'But I bet you don't have a bank at home like the Banco Rata. This bank is famous. If you are a rat with money, they will bank it for you and ask no questions. Dirty money, clean money, they don't care. This is the bank you come to if you have secrets you want to keep. They ask no questions, and they don't like anyone else to ask questions either.'

'But what about the **police**?' I said. 'What about the **government**? Why don't they close this place down?'

José laughed. He laughed so hard he began to cough and splutter and he had to sit down on the ground to catch his breath.

'Ah, that's a very funny joke, my friend,' he said as his laughter and coughing began to subside, 'a very funny joke. The police and the government, they are the biggest crooks of all!'

José laughed again, and that started him coughing again. As I waited for him to recover, I thought to myself that maybe Lima wasn't so different from my home town. After all, Kurt's last evil scheme was cooked up with the help of the Mayor and the old Chief of Police.

'So what do we do, then?' I asked José as the four of us stared back at the bank. 'What's **your** plan?'

José led us over to a shadowed doorway across from the bank. It belonged to an old biscuit shop that had long since closed down. We all crowded into the doorway and sat down. From the darkened shadows in the corner of the doorway, we could see the entrance to the bank but no one could see us.

'Well, my friends,' said José, 'here is my plan: we wait.'

'We wait?' said Spencer.

'We wait,' said José.

Every good policerat knows how to operate a stakeout, and I am the best policerat in the world. A stakeout is where you hide somewhere waiting for the bad guys to show up. It can take an hour, or it can take a week.

To run a good stakeout you need patience. You need to pay attention. You need to be very quiet and very observant. But you need more important things, too.

'Patrick,' I said, after we had been waiting and watching for fifteen minutes, 'we need coffee and we need doughnuts.'

Coffee and doughnuts — the essential ingredients of any good stakeout. The coffee keeps you awake, and the doughnuts ... well, the doughnuts just taste good. Doughnuts are perfect for every occasion, really, but for stakeouts they are more than perfect.

José gave some directions, and Patrick nipped off to get the supplies. While he was away I suddenly remembered that a good detective always keeps a record of any stakeout, so I took out my notebook and pen and began. This is what I wrote:

3.30 pm: Stakeout began 15 minutes ago. We are waiting for evidence of Kurt Remarque.

3.45 pm: Nothing.

4.00 pm: Nothing.

4.15 pm: Patrick returns with coffee and doughnuts. I can't believe it took so long.

4.30 pm: I like these doughnuts, especially the pineapple ones. However, I am saving one for later in case I need it.

4.45 pm: Nothing.

5.00 pm: Nothing.

5.01 pm: I am eating the last doughnut.

5.07 pm: Three rats enter the bank. None of them is K.R.

5.15 pm: We need more doughnuts, but Patrick won't go back. He says the shop is too far away. He is so selfish.

5.30 pm: Nothing.

5.45 pm: What a waste of time. José has fallen asleep.

5.48 pm: **WHAT ON EARTH WAS THAT???**

I dropped my notebook and shook José awake.

'José! José!' I said. 'Did you see that?'

'See what?' said José.

'That ... that ... **thing!** I said. 'It just walked into the bank.'

'What are you talking about, my friend?' said José. 'I saw nothing.'

'That's because you were **asleep!** I said indignantly. 'You should **never** sleep on a stakeout.'

'**I** saw it,' said Patrick.

'So did **I**,' said Spencer. 'It was like a rat, only even bigger and even uglier.'

'What do you mean even uglier?' I said. 'Are you suggesting that rats are ugly?'

'Look in a mirror some time,' said Spencer.

'Hey!' I said.

'My friends, my friends,' said José, turning to us. 'This

is no time for fighting among ourselves. Be calm, and tell me what you saw. What did this creature look like?'

'Well,' said Patrick, 'it was sort of big and sort of ugly, and it had a **really** big head …'

José sat up straighter, and his whiskers twitched. 'How big was this head?' he whispered.

'THAT big!' I said, pointing to the bank entrance.

José turned and stared.

The creature was coming back out of the bank.

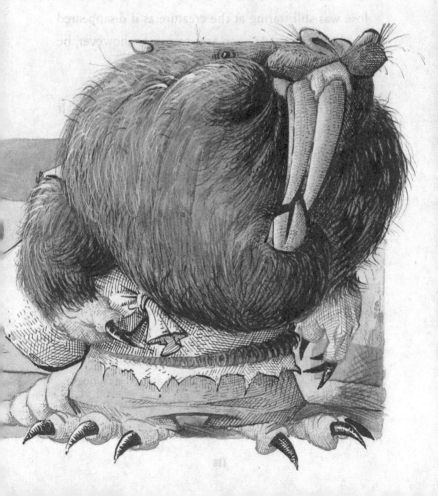

It was big — much bigger than a rat. It had dark fur, and short powerful legs with thick, dangerous-looking claws. Its tail was much shorter than a rat's, and its ears were tiny. But the thing you noticed most was its head, which looked almost as big as the rest of its body. It had tiny eyes tucked away in the middle of a giant pudding of a face, and two huge sharp yellowing front teeth. It trudged out of the bank clutching a bag under one of its muscular arms.

José was still staring at the creature as it disappeared around the corner. As soon as it was gone, however, he sprang into action.

'**Quick!**' he said. 'We must follow it.'

'Why?' said Spencer. 'That's not Kurt Remarque. It doesn't even look anything like him.'

'That is true, my friend,' said José, 'but I will tell you what that creature is. It is a **tuco-tuco**.'

We all sat there in silence.

'Okay,' I said at last. 'I'll ask it: **what is a tuco-tuco?**'

'Believe me, you don't want to know,' said José. 'But where a tuco-tuco goes, trouble will surely follow. There is no rodent meaner, tougher or more dangerous than a tuco-tuco, and you almost never see them here in the streets of Lima.'

'So why on earth should we **follow** it?' said Spencer.

'Because if your Kurt Remarque is as evil as you say he is, then I will bet my last peso that this tuco-tuco is mixed up with him somehow. It is too much of a coincidence,' said José, heading off down the alley in the direction the tuco-tuco went, 'there is an old saying in Peru. **If you can't follow the money, follow the tuco-tuco.'**

12
THE TAIL

If there is one thing every policerat knows how to do almost as well as a stakeout, it's a tail.

A tail, of course, is when you are following someone without letting them know you are there. The biggest difference between a tail and a stakeout is that there are no doughnuts involved in a tail. Pity, really, but it is too hard to walk, watch and eat at the same time.

We followed that tuco-tuco for **miles** — or at least it seemed like miles. At first, it was easy. The streets were so crowded with humans that there were plenty of places to hide and still keep up with our target. Just to be on the safe side, we all took turns walking in the front of our group, so that every time the tuco-tuco looked behind him he would see someone different and not realise he was being followed. As it turned out, though, he hardly ever turned around. He just kept trudging on. Maybe it was too much trouble to turn that huge head of his.

It got harder when we reached the outskirts of town.

The crowds thinned out and the streets grew longer and quieter. Eventually we had to hide around corners, and then peek out carefully in time to see him disappear around the next corner. Then we would rush up to that corner and one of us would carefully peek around again.

It worked for several blocks. But by now the sun was starting to go down and long shadows stretched across the roads. I was starting to wonder how much longer this tail was going to last and whether it would turn out to be a wild goose chase.

'My turn,' said Patrick, when we reached yet another corner. We all crouched down behind a building in the shadows. Patrick slowly poked his head around the corner. He was quiet for a few moments.

'**Whoops,**' he said.

Now, as a very experienced policerat I can tell you that **whoops** is not a good word to hear during a tail. 'There he goes' is a much better thing to hear, or even 'Quick, hurry up' or 'left at the next corner'. But **whoops** almost never means good news — and it certainly didn't on this occasion.

'What do you mean **whoops**?' said Spencer.

'He's gone,' said Patrick.

We all stepped around the corner and into the next street. It was empty.

Well, not really empty, to be strictly accurate. There were two humans walking along carrying baskets. There was a truck parked in front of a furniture shop. There was a nasty-looking yellow dog sleeping on the pavement. There were two large metal bins and a stack of old boxes and a small pile of dirt. But there were no tuco-tucos.

'He **is** gone', said Spencer.

'I **told** you,' said Patrick.

'We've lost him,' I said.

'No, we haven't,' said José.

He led us down the street, under the truck (where we hid until the two humans were out of sight), tiptoeing around the sleeping dog and past the bins and boxes until we arrived at the small pile of dirt.

'See?' he said triumphantly.

I looked down. Next to the pile of dirt was a small, perfectly formed hole.

'Down there?' I asked. 'You think he's gone **down there?'**

'I **know** he's gone down there,' José replied.

'And you expect us to crawl down there in the dark and go after him?' said Spencer.

'Not that we're afraid,' added Patrick.

'Listen, my friends,' said José. 'Let me tell you about these tuco-tucos. They live most of their lives underground, digging long, deep tunnels through the earth. These tunnels can go on for miles. They use their claws to dig through the earth and their big front teeth to chew the roots of trees away, then they push it all behind them with their claws and feet. Tuco-tucos are the best diggers in all of Peru — probably in all of the world.'

'So this **must** be a tuco-tuco tunnel,' I said, staring at the hole with the neat little mound of dirt beside it. 'But where do you think it leads, José?'

'It leads to where they live, my friend. These tuco-tucos, they are like bandits. They come into the city to steal things from hard-working rats like me then they carry it away to their tunnels. They live in burrows underground.'

'So if these tuco-tucos are mixed up with Kurt Remarque somehow ...' Spencer began.

'Then we must follow them to their burrow,' said José, finishing her sentence for her. 'It will be very dangerous, because no tuco-tuco likes a stranger coming into their burrow. But I think we must find out what is happening, no?'

I looked at Spencer, and then at Patrick. They looked a little nervous.

'You're right, José,' I said. 'We've come this far, and this is our only clue since we arrived. We can't give up now.'

'That's the spirit!' said José. 'Are you all ready?'

'Sure,' said Spencer.

'No worries,' said Patrick.

'There's just one more thing,' I said, as José began lowering himself gingerly into the hole. 'Why are they called tuco-tucos?'

'I hope you never find out,' said José, and he dropped down into the hole and disappeared into the darkness.

****

I couldn't see my whiskers in front of my face. In fact, I couldn't see **anything** in front of my face. Let's be honest — I couldn't see my face.

'I can't see **anything**,' I whispered.

'**Shhh** ... they'll hear you,' came José's reply from somewhere in front of me.

We were stumbling along through the darkness in search of the tuco-tuco. The tunnel was narrow and low. It was fine for Spencer and Patrick, who were much smaller than me, and I think José was travelling well too, because he must have done this sort of thing before. But I kept knocking my head against rocks and pieces of tree root sticking out of the walls of the tunnel.

'How do you know we're going the right way?' I whispered again.

'Haven't you noticed?' said José. 'This tunnel only goes in one direction. Just keep following me and keep quiet — we don't want them to hear us coming if we can help it.'

'Ouch!' I replied. That was another rock.

We kept muddling along in the darkness. It was hard even to tell whether the tunnel was going straight or turning around. For all I knew, we could have been going in circles.

Suddenly I came crashing to a stop. I had hit some sort of wall in front of me. It was large, soft and furry in places. Then I realised — it was José. He had stopped. No sooner had I realised that, than I felt something knock into me from behind.

'**OOMPH!**' came Spencer's voice as she ran straight into me.

'**Ow!**' came the distant sound of Patrick as he crashed into Spencer.

'Look,' said José.

I leant over José's shoulder and looked. A faint shaft of light was coming from somewhere further down the tunnel.

'What is that?' I whispered.

'That must be their burrow' said José. 'We must be **very** careful now.'

We began to move very slowly down the tunnel towards the source of light. Now we could see where we were going, which made it easier. The earth was brown and a little damp and the floor looked very worn, as if hundreds of tuco-tuco feet had tramped up and down it for years. Every now and then we would have to duck to get past a tree root sticking out of the roof or one of the walls. At least I wasn't walking straight into them now.

The light got brighter and brighter and the tunnel began to get a little wider. Other, smaller tunnels joined it from the sides, but still we could see no tuco-tucos anywhere. We were alone, with only the sound of our footsteps for company.

José began to slow down even more. Then he moved quickly over to the left-hand side of the tunnel, into the shadow of a large outcrop of rock.

'See?' he said.

The tunnel ahead of us had opened up into a huge cave. The light we had been following came from dozens of small candles that had been set into little hollows dug in the walls. In the middle of the huge room, a pot of some sort of soup was bubbling away on a fire. There were little groups of tuco-tucos everywhere. Some were sleeping, others were munching on hunks of bread. The one we had been following was moving from group to group, handing out something from the bag he had been carrying. I leant forward to look a little closer and I saw that it was money.

'Do you think that's Kurt Remarque's money?' said Spencer from behind me.

'I'll bet it is,' I said excitedly. 'They're up to **something**, that's for sure.'

'But **what?**' said Spencer, peering more closely at the scene in front of us. All of the tuco-tucos had begun to gather around the one with the money bag now. He was talking to them and I strained to catch what he was saying. I couldn't seem to make sense of his words, and suddenly I realised he was speaking Spanish.

I managed to catch a few words. They sounded like airaperto, gorda and rata blanca.

'What is he saying?' I whispered to José, who was leaning forward as well to try to catch the words.

'I can't quite hear,' said José. 'I think he said **the airport**, and something about **a fat white rat.**'

'**A fat white rat?**' I said.

'**KURT REMARQUE!!**' burst out Patrick. Very loudly. **Too** loudly. You wouldn't think such a small mouse would have such a big voice, but he does.

Every tuco-tuco in the cave froze. Then they looked in our direction. Could they see us, hiding behind the rock? We stood very, very still, our hearts beating frantically.

There was silence in the cave. Not a thing moved. Then we heard it — softly at first, like a faint whisper.

Tuco-tuco ... tuco-tuco ... tuco-tuco.

The tuco-tucos were making a noise. It started low, like a sort of chanting. It was as if they were simply saying their name. Then it got louder and louder, and they began scratching their sharp claws back and forth on the ground.

TUCO-TUCO ... TUCO-TUCO ... TUCO-TUCO!!

'**What's happening?**' I yelled over the noise.

'**Now** you see why they are called tuco-tucos,' said José. 'This is the noise they make when they are scared or angry. It is meant to scare away strangers.'

'Is this all they do?' I yelled. 'Just make this awful racket?'

'Sometimes,' hollered José. 'But sometimes, if they get really angry, they **attack**.'

TUCO-TUCO ... TUCO-TUCO ... TUCO-TUCO!!

The chanting was faster and faster now, and the furious scratching of their claws in the dirt sounded like a million fingernails running down a million blackboards.

How angry is REALLY angry? I wondered as I covered my ears against the chanting and scratching.

At that very moment, the tuco-tucos **charged!** They were heading straight for us, their claws drumming over the earth and their huge teeth bared.

It was time to be brave.

'RUN!!' yelled Spencer.

Boy, did we run.

13
NOT QUITE ALL IS REVEALED

Back down the tunnel we went, trying to stay on our feet as we stumbled through the growing darkness. I could hear the shrill sound of the tuco-tucos chanting their name over and over as they thundered along behind us.

'They're getting closer,' I yelled, 'and I don't like the look of those claws.'

'This way!' said Spencer urgently.

'**Which** way?' I said, slowing a little and looking around. 'It's too dark. I can't —'

Someone yanked on my collar and I felt myself being tugged sideways. It was Spencer. She dragged me into one of the smaller tunnels that ran off to the side. José and Patrick followed and the four of us crouched in the darkness a few feet down the tunnel.

The thundering, screeching, chanting crowd of tuco-tucos came closer and closer, and then they were right next to us. They charged down the main tunnel and right past the entrance to the small one we were hiding in. The noise faded away and they were gone.

'Phew!' said Patrick the Magnificent. 'That was close. What do we do now?'

'We must keep moving,' said José. 'It would be dangerous to wait here, my friends. Sooner or later they will come back.'

'So which way do we go?' I asked. 'If we head back out into the main tunnel, we're sure to meet up with the tuco-tucos again.'

'Well,' said Spencer, 'I reckon that

leaves us with one option. Let's find out where this little tunnel leads to.'

With Spencer leading the way, we began moving down the narrow tunnel. It was dark, of course, and this tunnel had lots of twists and turns, so we had to creep along carefully, feeling for obstacles up ahead.

It wasn't long before our narrow path became clogged with grass, roots and bushes. It was like pushing your way through a jungle.

Finally, we turned yet another corner and saw another shaft of light filtering through the greenery. It **had** to be coming from the open air.

Sure enough, after a few more metres, the tunnel sloped sharply uphill and we emerged into a clump of weeds and bushes.

'I know where we are,' said José, looking around. 'This isn't far from the river.'

We sat down in the shade of the bushes to catch our breath and think about our next move. José produced a small brown flask from the inside of his poncho and passed it around.

'Here, my friends, have some. It is naranjilla juice — very good for you.'

Spencer, Patrick and I all tasted some. It was bitter and strong, but rather nice. It tasted a bit like oranges.

'Well, I suppose we need a **plan**,' I said after a moment. 'Spencer, **you** always like a good **plan**, don't you? What now?'

Spencer frowned at me. 'There's **nothing** wrong with a good **plan**,' she said. 'I just don't seem to have one on me at the moment.'

'Well, let's take stock,' I said. 'José, what exactly did you hear down in that cave?'

José took another swig of his naranjilla juice and leant back on a clump of weeds.

'All I heard was that tuco-tuco talking about a fat white rat. And I am pretty sure he also said something about the airport. But my ears are not so good these days, my friends. Too much loud music and singing when I was a young rat.'

'**I** heard something,' said Patrick out of the blue.

'**You** heard something?' I asked. 'Why didn't you say so **before**? Quickly, what was it?'

'Well, that's just it,' said Patrick. 'I don't speak their language, do I? So I heard something, but I have absolutely no idea what it meant.'

I sighed. It was a false clue, leading nowhere.

'Thanks for nothing, Patrick,' I said grumpily.

'Wait a minute, Patrick,' said José. 'Can you tell me what they **sounded** like, the words you heard?'

'What they **sounded** like?' said Patrick.

'Yes,' said José, sitting up a little straighter. 'Never mind what the words mean — just tell me what they **sounded** like.'

'I'll try,' said Patrick. 'It was the first bit I heard most clearly. Let me think ...'

The little mouse closed his eyes to help him concentrate.

'It was something like ... something like manyarna porla manyarna, temprano, hay kay ray you neernos ... and then a word like airport, the bit you heard.'

'Say it again,' said José. 'More slowly.'

Patrick repeated himself carefully, taking his time over each unfamiliar word.

... manyarna porla manyarna, temprano, hay kay ray you neernos...

'Yes!' said José excitedly. 'Yes, it must be. It think what you heard was the Spanish for **tomorrow morning we meet early**. Did it sound like this? Mañana por la mañana, temprano, hay que reuniros?'

'That's it!' said Patrick.

'Perfect,' said José. 'I myself heard that tuco-tuco mention the airport and a fat white rat. It all fits, my friends.'

'You know,' I said to Spencer as we got to our feet, 'I do believe we have a **plan**. Early tomorrow morning, we go to the airport, and if we don't find Kurt Remarque there, then I'll eat my hat.'

'What, **again?**' said Spencer. 'But what do we do if he **is** there? What then?'

'I'll get back to you on that bit,' I said.

****

There was a sort of smudgy grey mist hanging over the airport when we got there early the next morning.

We'd spent a pleasant night at José's place, sleeping on the piles of hessian sacks. We hadn't talked much. It had been a long day.

In the morning, after a breakfast of fruit and bread and some more of that naranjilla juice, we hitched a ride to the airport on a van loaded with bananas. I must confess I even sampled one on the way. It was a bit too green for my liking.

'Tell me, José,' I said as we bumped along the road, 'do they have any special kinds of doughnuts in Peru?'

José never got to answer, because just then we swerved around a corner into the airport driveway.

The truck drove into a big hangar on the edge of the

runway, and parked in a corner. We climbed out and gathered next to one of the back wheels.

'What now?' said Spencer.

'We spread out,' I said. 'One building at a time. If you come across any tuco-tucos, or if you see Kurt Remarque, just whistle. Nice and loud. Then we all come running and ...'

'And what?' asked Patrick.

'And I'll tell you when I work something out,' I answered. 'Patrick, you go over to the main passenger terminal and see what's happening. Spencer, try that row of warehouses over there. José, you head over to the main runway and see if there's anything suspicious going on.'

'Certainly, my friend,' said José. 'Where will **you** be?'

'I'll be right here, checking out this warehouse,' I said.

We all split up and headed in different directions. I wandered down the aisles of the warehouse, passing crates of different fruits and vegetables ready to be loaded onto planes and sent around the world. There were pineapples, passionfruit, bananas (of course), apples, oranges ... no doughnuts. I know a doughnut isn't technically a fruit, but I had them on my mind.

I got to the end of the warehouse and I had seen nothing even slightly suspicious. There was one banana that was a slightly unusual shape, but I didn't count that.

I slipped out through a large sliding door and found myself on the edge of a small runway. There was a little plane sitting there — the kind with propellers instead of engines. I looked at it and then looked away and then looked back again. There was something not quite right about it. **What was it?**

I looked at it more carefully. Two wings, with two sets of propellers on each. Two wheels at the front, and one at the back. Six windows down the side of the plane's body, and a door that was open, ready for the passengers. There was a set of six steps leading down from the door so that the passengers could climb aboard.

At the back of the plane was a smaller opening, which looked like the place where you put all the bags and boxes and other luggage. There was a small rope ladder leading from it down to the ground.

Wait a minute! A rope ladder? Leading into the luggage compartment? Who needs a **rope ladder** to put bags into the hold of a plane?

I looked more closely at the ladder. As I watched, something ran out from the grass at the edge of the runway and shimmied up the ladder. Something dark and quick.

I looked back to the spot where this dark, quick shape had come from, and there, in the grass on the runway's edge, was a small pile of dirt.

It must have been a **tuco-tuco!**

I stood very still and watched carefully and sure enough, another dark shape dashed across from the runway's edge and disappeared up the ladder. This time I could see that it **was** a tuco-tuco — the small muscular body and the huge ugly head were unmistakable.

I stood there for five minutes and three more tuco-tucos ran up that ladder. Then for another five minutes nothing happened, then I heard a strange whining metallic noise and the sound of engines spluttering into life. I looked across and the propellers of the plane had begun to spin.

Come on, OcKo, I thought to myself, **Do something!**

I knew there were tuco-tucos on that plane, but I didn't know what else I would find. But I am a police detective — the best and the bravest in the world. I **had** to find out.

I whistled as loud and as long as I could, but I couldn't be sure that any of my friends would hear me over the sound of the plane's engines. Then I started running across the tarmac, heading for the rope ladder.

There was nowhere to hide and no reason to slow down and look around: I just put my head down and ran for it. The propellers were spinning faster and faster, but the plane still wasn't going anywhere; it was just vibrating a little as I climbed up the rope ladder. I made it all the way to the top, and then very, very slowly I lifted my head to look into the plane.

There were at least a dozen tuco-tucos in the luggage compartment, but luckily they all had their backs to me. They were listening to someone who was yelling at them over the sound of the engines. I could just make out the words from where I stood, clinging to the top rung of the rope ladder.

This plane follows the route of the Rio Ucayali and then the Rio Apurimac,' said the voice, 'and it will take us high into the Andes. We will march all day, until we reach the Nevado Mismi.'

I was frozen to the spot. I couldn't believe what I was hearing. Don't get me wrong — I didn't care about all the places the voice was talking about. I knew there were probably some good clues in it all, but that wasn't what interested me, as I hung on for dear life to a rope ladder dangling from a plane. No, what really caught my attention and froze me to the spot was the voice itself; the deep, dangerous tone of the voice. It could only belong to one rat: **Kurt Remarque.**

'No questions,' boomed the voice. 'I will explain everything when we get there. Now, are we all on board? Twelve, thirteen, fourteen ... yes, that's a good-sized team. We're about to take off, so release the ladder and close the compartment before the pilot notices us.'

Release the ladder? **Release the ladder???** That would be the ladder I was clinging to, I assumed.

The noise of the engines got louder. The plane was beginning to taxi along the runway, ready for takeoff.

The tuco-tuco nearest to the back of the crowd turned around to undo the rope ladder, and found himself staring straight into my eyes.

I think it's fair to say that he was surprised.

Tuco-tuco! Tuco-tuco! Tuco-tuco! The tuco-tuco screeched out in alarm at the same time as he kicked out at me with his powerful legs. I clung to the rope, which began swinging from side to side as the plane picked up speed.

Soon, a whole bunch of tuco-tucos had surrounded the entrance, all of them screeching loudly. They were kicking at the rope ladder, trying to hit me or at least to dislodge the ladder. Others had grabbed hold of the compartment door and were trying to shut it, but it kept jamming on the ladder and blowing back open again.

The friction of the door was starting to fray the rope of the ladder. The plane was moving really fast now, hurtling down the runway with me and the rope ladder flapping behind it.

The tuco-tucos stared down at me, snarling and screeching. The wind was so strong that I was almost blown off the ladder, but I clung on desperately.

I felt the plane lurch into the air and I realised we were airborne.

As I stared up at the gang of angry tuco-tucos, a

different face suddenly appeared among them. It was a white face. A fat, white rat-face with tiny pink eyes. **Kurt Remarque!**

For a split second, Kurt Remarque's eyes locked on mine. I saw surprise on his face. Surprise and then anger. He reached a fat white arm through the crowd of tuco-tucos, grabbed the door of the luggage compartment, and wrenched it shut.

The last thing I saw before the door closed was the furious face of Kurt Remarque, his whiskers twisting with rage. Then the door slammed, severing the top of the rope ladder, and I was falling through the Peruvian sky . . .

14
COME FLY WITH ME

'Ocko! Ocko, wake up!'

I opened my eyes, and found myself staring into the worried face of Spencer. I tried a quick smile, but it hurt too much, so I stopped.

'He's awake,' came the sound of Spencer's voice.

I realised I must have closed my eyes again, so I opened them. Spencer still looked worried.

'Ocko, how are you feeling?' she asked, leaning over and peering into my face.

Considering I had just fallen out of a plane, I thought that was a rather stupid question, but it would probably be rude to point that out.

'What a stupid question!' I yelled.

See, sometimes my mouth doesn't quite listen to what my brain is thinking.

'Try to sit up,' said Spencer, ignoring my rudeness.

I tried to sit up, and immediately wished I hadn't. My whole body hurt. My tail hurt, my head hurt, even my whiskers hurt. It felt like I had spent half an hour in

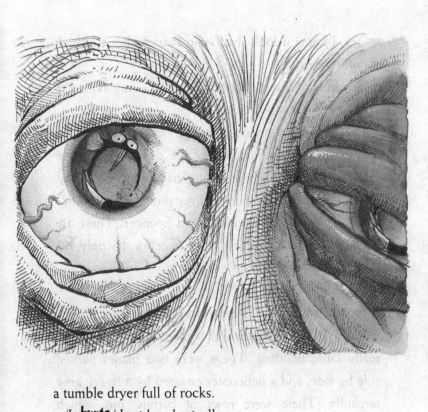

a tumble dryer full of rocks.

'It **hurts**,' I said pathetically.

'**What** hurts?' said Spencer.

'**Everything** hurts,' I replied through gritted teeth as I sat up and looked around.

Spencer still looked worried and so did Patrick, who was right behind her. Even José, who was usually so calm and relaxed, was rubbing his hands together and moving anxiously from foot to foot.

Then I looked down at myself to assess the damage.

'*AAARRGGhHH!*

That was me making that sound.

'Yes, I know it looks bad,' said Patrick, 'but we think it's only superficial.'

'Superficial?' I said. **Superficial?** This is my **fur** we're talking about. Or what's left of it.'

I gazed down at my poor body: I looked like a poodle. Part of me had fur and part of me didn't. There were huge bare patches where the fur had been worn away, leaving grazes and cuts all over my pink, exposed skin.

'Oh, don't be such a **baby**,' said Spencer. 'There are no broken bones, nothing needs stitches. It's only **fur** — it'll grow back.'

'Probably,' added Patrick.

Probably! Just what I needed to hear.

I looked around again and realised we were inside a really large building. There were two planes parked side by side, and a helicopter covered by a heavy grey tarpaulin. There were rows of barrels, too, which looked like they were full of some kind of fuel. We must still be at the airport.

'How long have I been unconscious?' I mumbled.

'Just a few minutes,' said Spencer. 'We carried you in here from outside.'

'I guess I lost my fur when I hit the ground,' I said ruefully, rubbing at the sore spots on my arms and my back.

'You sure did,' said Patrick. 'You looked like a bowling ball rolling down that runway. It's a miracle you survived.'

'It was no miracle,' I said. 'It was training — **years** of training. I've done that a **million times** in policerat training school.'

'I think he's delirious,' said Spencer. 'He's imagining things.'

'Very funny,' I snapped, even though it wasn't.

'So tell me, my friend,' said José. 'Did you see anything before you fell out of the plane?'

Suddenly it all came back to me. I jumped to my feet, forgetting the pain for a moment.

'Kurt Remarque!' I said. 'He was on the plane with fourteen tuco-tucos. We were right! He **is** here and he **is** up to something.'

'What?' said all three of them together.

'What is he up to?' added Spencer.

'I have no idea,' I said despondently. 'I fell before I had a chance to find out. But I **did** hear something about where they're going.'

'Excellent,' said José. 'Tell me what you heard and perhaps I will know this place.'

'Okay, let me think,' I said. 'He mentioned two places, and they both started with Rio.'

'Rio is the word for river,' said José, 'can you think of the names of these two rivers?'

'No ... no, I can't remember,' I said. 'But he **did** say they would go high into the Andes.'

'Ah, the Andes, this is good,' said José. 'So they are heading for the mountains. What else? Did he say where exactly in the mountains?'

'Yes,' I said, concentrating as hard as I could. 'It was some place called ... called ... called ...'

José was hanging on my every word, but I wasn't giving him much to go on. I closed my eyes and imagined I was back on the plane, clinging to the ladder and trying to hear Kurt Remarque's words over the sound of the engines.

'This is going to sound crazy,' I went on, 'but I think the name of the place sounded a bit like **never miss me**.'

'Never miss me?' said Patrick. 'I think your brain must have broken in the fall. Never miss me? What kind of place is **that?**'

But I looked at José, and I could see that he was thinking hard. He held up his hand for silence.

'Could it be? Surely not,' he said, as if he were talking to himself. Then he looked at me. 'My friend, do you think perhaps he said Nevado Mismi?'

'**That's it!**' I cried, slapping my hands together and immediately wishing I hadn't. (They hurt.) '**That's** the place. Weird name.'

'It is a strange name, but a **beautiful** place,' said José. 'But why on earth would this Kurt Remarque go there? That I do not know, unless ...'

José stopped talking and went back to thinking.

'What?' I asked.

'Nevado Mismi,' said José, 'is a cliff, a beautiful cliff,

148

high up in the Andes Mountains where the air is pure and the water is crystal clear. There is a tiny, tiny waterfall at this place — just a trickle of water, really. The snow melts from high in the mountains and some of it travels underground to this special place, where it starts a very long journey.'

'It sounds beautiful,' said Spencer, 'but why would someone like Kurt Remarque go there?'

'This is what worries me,' said José. 'But you must let me finish. There is a reason why this place is so special. The water that starts here, at Nevado Mismi, goes on a very long journey. An **amazing** journey, you might say, for it travels six thousand kilometres, right across the continent, until it flows into the Atlantic Ocean. It gets bigger and bigger and bigger, and more rivers and streams join with it, and before it reaches the ocean, it waters the mighty rainforests, it helps the crops grow, and it provides life and food to all the people along the way. It keeps the world alive.'

I had absolutely no idea what he was talking about, but Spencer's eyes were wide.

'Are you saying what I **think** you're saying?' she said. 'Do you mean to tell me that this little trickle of water turns into ... the **Amazon**?'

'That is **exactly** what I am saying, my friend,' said José. 'Nevado Mismi is the source of the Amazon, the greatest and most important river in the world.'

'The Amazon!' said Patrick.

'That's right,' said José. 'There is more water flowing down the Amazon than any other river in the world. You know, they say that the rainforests that grow because of this river make one-fifth of all the oxygen in the world. That means the fact that you are breathing right now is thanks to this river.'

'And Kurt Remarque is on his way to the source of this river?' I said. 'This can't be good.'

'No way,' said Spencer.

'Not good,' said Patrick.

'And he said nothing on the plane about why he was going?' asked José.

'Not a word,' I said.

'Well,' said José, 'there is only one thing to do, my friends. We must follow him. And we haven't a moment to lose.'

'Yes, but how?' I said. 'His plane left ages ago. We'll **never** catch him.'

'There must be **other** planes going to Nevado Mismi,' said José. 'Wait here for me. I will ask around.'

José slipped out the door of the hangar. While we waited for him, Spencer dressed my grazes and cuts with little pink strips of sticking plaster from a first-aid kit she found in the corner of the hangar. It made me look even more ridiculous, but at least I felt a little better.

As she patched me up, we talked about what Kurt could possibly be up to.

'It sounds bad to me,' said Patrick. 'If this never-miss-me place is the source of the Amazon, you can bet Kurt wants to ruin it and he's hired those tuco-tucos to help him.'

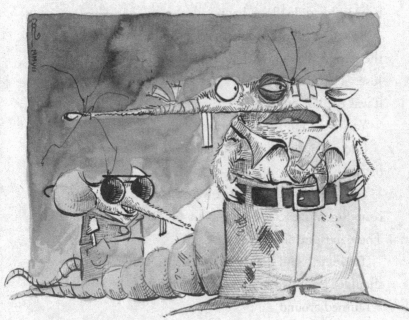

'Yes,' I said, 'but how? What's he going to do?'

'One thing's for sure,' said Spencer. 'If Kurt's involved, it is going to be some sort of evil plot.'

'Yes,' I said, 'but it will be a **stupid** evil plot. Remember last time, when he tried to poison the whole town's water supply, but the men who did it used nothing but red cordial?'

'Wait a minute!' said Patrick. 'You don't think he's going to poison the **whole river**, do you?'

'Not very likely,' I said. 'I don't know how you could

do something like that, and what would be the point, anyway?'

We were still thinking when José came back into the hangar. He didn't look happy.

'I went to find an old friend of mine who works at the airport. I'm afraid the news is bad, my friends,' said José. 'The plane that Kurt Remarque stowed away on, it was the last one this week.'

'You're kidding,' said Spencer.

'I do not joke,' said José. 'The next one is not for six days.'

'Six days!' I said. 'We can't wait that long. In six days, Kurt Remarque could get up to **all sorts** of mischief. There must be another way.'

'There is,' said Patrick. He was looking over my shoulder towards the back of the hangar.

I turned around.

'Yeah, great,' I said sarcastically. 'We'll just jump in one of those planes and fly there ourselves. I don't know why I didn't think of it straight away.'

Patrick sighed theatrically and rolled his eyes. 'Don't be **ridiculous**, Ocko,' he said. 'Mice can't fly planes.'

'Well, I'm glad you worked **that** one out,' I said.

'Of course,' said Patrick the Magnificent. 'I meant the helicopter.'

There was silence for ten seconds. I tried to decide whether Patrick was joking, or whether he was insane. I couldn't decide.

'The helicopter?' I said at last.

'You bet,' said Patrick, grinning. 'I know all about helicopters. Two sticks and two pedals, that's all you need to fly one of those things. That's **four** things you need to operate, and there are **four** of us. We can do it easily!'

That was when I knew he wasn't joking. Which left only one option.

'You're insane,' I said. 'I've lost enough of my fur today. If it's okay with you, I'd rather stay alive.'

'No, listen,' said Patrick the Magnificent. 'I've read all about how you fly a helicopter. There's a stick that makes the engine go, another one that makes you go forwards, backwards and to the sides, and two pedals to tilt left and right. All we need to do is start it up, then everyone takes one control each, and I'll lead the way. José can tell us the direction and we'll be fine.'

'I think I know how to get there,' said José. 'We'll just follow the rivers back to their source — it's easy.'

'What else can we do?' said Spencer. 'I say it's worth a try.'

'**I can't believe I'm hearing this!**' I yelled. 'Two rats and two mice are going to fly a **helicopter** over the **Andes mountains** to find the source of the **Amazon**? You're all **CRAZY**!'

'Well, what's **your** plan, then?' said Spencer. 'Sit here and do nothing?'

That sounded pretty good to me, actually. I looked

at my three friends. I looked at the helicopter, sitting there under the tarpaulin. I thought about Kurt Remarque and his evil band of tuco-tucos, hurtling through the air on their way to carry out some terrible mission. How do I get myself into these situations?

'Tell me again how you operate that thing,' I said to Patrick.

Five minutes later, the tarpaulin was lying on the ground, and we were inside the helicopter.

'Okay,' said Patrick, 'let's go through this one more time.'

Spencer and José were on the floor of the helicopter cabin, each of them standing on a pedal. Patrick was holding on to something that looked like a giant handbrake between the two seats, and I was in the pilot's seat with my arms wrapped around a huge stick that went backwards and forwards, up and down. I think he'd given me the most complicated job.

'Right,' said Patrick. 'We turn this thing on, I pull back on my lever to speed up the engine, and then, Ocko, you steer us out of this hangar. If we start going to the left, I'll tell José to press down on the right pedal, and if we start going too far to the right, I'll tell Spencer to press down on the left pedal. Easy.'

'Yes,' I said, 'there is just one small detail. I can't see a thing out of the windscreen.'

'Is that a problem?' said Spencer.

'OF COURSE it's a problem!' I shouted. This is the

most stupid thing I've ever agreed to do, but if we're going to do it, don't you think we need to be able to **see where we're going?**

'I suppose he has a point,' said Patrick.

'Will this help?' said José. He had stepped off his pedal, and he was pulling a thick helicopter manual out of a pocket in the door.

'What do you want me to do, **read** that thing?' I asked.

'No, no, my friend,' said José. 'Stand on it.' He heaved it up onto the seat and I climbed on top of it. If I stood on tiptoes and jumped in the air I could just about see the open door of the hangar in front of me.

'I guess it will have to do,' I said. 'Let's get this over and done with.'

I leant over and flicked a switch on the control

panel of the helicopter. The huge rotor blade hummed and then slowly began to move.

'Everyone ready?' yelled Patrick over the growing noise.

'Ready as we'll ever be,' shouted Spencer.

Patrick pulled back on his lever, and the blades of the helicopter began to whirr faster and faster. The helicopter shuddered and jerked twice, and then I felt it lift off the ground.

We immediately pitched forward towards the door and then veered off to the left. I pulled back on my lever and the nose of the helicopter lifted into the air.

'Right! Right!' yelled Patrick.

José stomped down hard on his pedal and the helicopter veered crazily to the right.

'Left! Left!' screamed Patrick.

Spencer pushed down and we started heading for the left wall fast.

'Right!' yelled Patrick.

'Make up your mind!' yelled Spencer.

'Look out!' I yelled, pulling on my lever. We were heading for the right-hand corner of the roof.

The helicopter swayed crazily back and forth and pitched up and down inside the hangar. I tried to ignore Patrick as he yelled out, 'Right! Left! No, right! Up! Down! Watch out! What are you doing?' Every couple of seconds, I jumped up into the air and looked out the windscreen, then I tried to steer the bucking machine with my lever, pushing forward and steering left or right depending on what Spencer and José were doing below me.

I waited until we were briefly and accidentally in the middle of the hangar again, then I yelled, 'More power!' to Patrick. He pulled back on his control and the engine roared. I pushed forward on my stick and the helicopter shot out of the hangar door like a dragonfly escaping from a bottle.

We were in the open, with sky above us!

I pulled back on the lever just before the nose of the helicopter hit the ground, and we lurched higher into the air.

'WHOOPEE!!' said Patrick. He clapped his hands in the air. 'It's working! It's working!'

Well, it **was** working. But what Patrick had obviously forgotten is that you can't clap your hands and hold on to a helicopter lever at the same time. Honestly, I'm not prejudiced against mice, but really, how dumb can you be? As soon as he let go of the lever the helicopter slowed and headed for the ground again.

'**EEEEEEKKK!**' said Patrick. I knew how he felt. He quickly grabbed the lever and pulled back on it, and we shuddered back up into the sky.

'What **on earth** is going on up there?' said Spencer.

'Sorry,' said Patrick, 'won't happen again.'

We were climbing higher and higher now, leaving the airport far behind us.

'Okay, what now?' I said, hopping up and down to check out the window.

'We must go southeast,' said José, 'and follow the rivers. They will lead us where we want to go.'

Southeast? I looked at all the dials on the dashboard in front of me. One of them was a compass. The needle was halfway between the 'W' and the 'N'. We were going the **wrong way**.

I hauled on the lever, and we began to slowly circle in the air. When the needle was pointing halfway between the 'S' and the 'E', I straightened up and tried to keep it reasonably level as we rattled along.

Spencer and José sat down on their pedals, taking care to keep them steady, and Patrick leant back on the lever so that we were travelling at a nice even pace.

After a while I looked through the window and saw a thick blue line snaking across the ground below us.

'I think I see a river!' I cried.

'Excellent, my friend,' said José. 'This will take you into the mountains. Just try not to hit one of them when we get there.'

So there we were — two mice and two rats flying through the air in a helicopter. Not bad, really.

Once we left the misty air of Lima behind, the sky was blue, the sun was warm, and a cool breeze blew in through one of the windows in the helicopter, which was slightly open. We even passed a couple of huge birds that looked like eagles, only really ugly. One of them looked through our window as we rattled past. He looked surprised, as well he might.

It wasn't long before I could just see, over the edge of the windscreen, some mountains looming up ahead.

They were huge and dark, except for the very tops, which were covered in snow.

'José!' I yelled over the sound of the engine. 'This looks bad. There are mountains ahead, and they are huge, with snow on top. We'll never get over them.'

I could hear José laughing. 'Don't worry, my friend,' he said calmly, 'we don't **need** to climb above them. We will land before then.'

'When?' I called. **'Where?'**

'Just follow the river as it goes into the mountains. Tell me when it disappears.'

I was becoming something of an expert at controlling the helicopter by now, so I dipped the nose down a bit as we flew and discovered that it gave me a

much better view of the scene in front of us.

The river we were following was smaller now, as it got closer to the foot of the mountain range. On either side of it were tiny villages, surrounded by green fields.

'There are hills below us now,' I called.

'This is good. We have reached the start of the beautiful Andes Mountains.' said José. 'You have done well. Just keep climbing a little higher, but remember, try not to hit them. This would not be good, my friend.'

Being a highly trained policerat, it came as no surprise to me to learn that hitting a mountain with a helicopter was not a good idea.

'Pull back on your lever, Patrick,' I yelled. He did, and we lifted a little higher as the ground rose up below us.

The snow-covered mountains still sat there in front of us, but now we were flying over smaller hills and valleys. Looking down, I couldn't really see a river at all any more.

'José! I don't know where I am, and I have no idea where I'm going,' I cried.

'Don't worry, my friend,' laughed José, 'just tell me what you can see.'

'Um ... the mountains ahead of us, some hills and valleys, lots of trees, and — oh, there goes another one of those ugly birds.'

'Okay,' said José. 'Can you see a valley, a nice green valley, with a wall of rock at one end of it?'

'Hang on.'

I pushed the nose of the helicopter down a bit further to see better. There were small hills and valleys all over the place, and they all looked the same. Then I saw it — an open green field surrounded by hills on all sides, except that one of the hills was bare rock, a sheer black cliff that rose up into the air like the side of a building.

'I think I see it, José!' I said. 'It's green and lush, but there's a cliff at the end of it.'

'Perfect!' said José excitedly. 'Now we must go closer, my friend. Get closer to the cliff, and tell me what you can see.'

'Ease back a bit, Patrick,' I said. 'We have to slow down.'

Patrick lowered his lever a little and I heard the sound change as the blades of the helicopter slowed down. I pulled back on my control and we were hanging in the sky now, hovering next to the cliff face. **Boy, were we getting good at this!**

'Okay, José,' I said. 'It's a solid cliff wall, very dark, and ... wait ... I can just make out something ...'

'What do you see?' José wanted to know.

'I think it's ... yes, it's a little trickle of water. A tiny waterfall.'

'Yes!' cried José. **This is it!** Nevado Mismi! This tiny trickle is the source of the mighty Amazon, the greatest river in the world! **We have arrived!**

163

'**Great!**' I said, but even as I said it I was thinking, '**Now, how do we land this thing?**'

'Is there any sign of Kurt Remarque?' said Spencer.

Kurt Remarque! I'd been so busy flying a helicopter towards some mountains I'd almost forgotten why we were there.

'Wait, I'll check,' I said, and I dipped the nose of the helicopter towards the ground to see if anyone was there.

For a brief moment, I could have sworn I saw some movement on the ground. Was it a tuco-tuco? But before I could take a closer look, I was distracted by something else.

I should probably pause here and tell you something I learnt that day — something I didn't really know before. Apparently, if you are hovering in the air in a helicopter, it is not a good idea to point the machine towards the ground. Helicopters are amazing things, and you can do a lot with them, but if you turn them too far and point them towards the ground, especially if you're not going very fast to begin with, there is a real danger that they will drop out of the sky like a stone.

We dropped out of the sky like a stone.

The thing that distracted me was Spencer, José and Patrick all screaming at the same time as we plummeted towards the ground.

I tried to pull back hard on the controls to lift the front of the helicopter. For a moment, nothing happened, then we came out of our dive, straightened up … and started heading straight for the cliff face!

That's when **I** started screaming too.

I swerved wildly to the left and felt a loud **CRUNCH!** as the back of the helicopter slammed against the cliff. It felt as if something had fallen off. We swerved back to the right and this time it was the nose of the helicopter that hit the cliff. A big crack shivered across the windscreen, one of the doors fell off and the engine stalled completely. **This can't be good**, I thought to myself as we started plummeting towards the ground again.

We hit the ground with a **CRASH** they must have heard back in Lima. Then the whole helicopter began tumbling and twisting over itself as we slid down a hill towards a clump of trees. Spencer, Patrick, José and I were thrown all over the place. I caught a glimpse of sky, then a glimpse of grass, and then a glimpse of the trees — just as we hit them.

The first couple of trees were small and we smashed straight through them. But the next ones were bigger and thicker and we were no match for them. There was a *THUD*, then a sort of splintering sound followed by a shower of leaves, and the helicopter came to a stop, hissing and moaning, upside down.

No one moved or said anything for several seconds. Then I heard a faint voice from somewhere above me.

'Nice parking, Ocko.' It was Spencer.

I looked up to see her clinging to the pedal above me. Patrick was clinging to her tail, swinging back and forth like the pendulum of a clock.

'Are you two okay?' I asked, checking myself over to make sure nothing was broken.

'Well,' said Spencer, 'it depends on your definition of **okay**, I guess. I'm hanging upside down in a helicopter with a mouse clinging to my tail. Apart from that, I couldn't be better. How about you?'

Just at that moment, Patrick let go and fell down beside me. Spencer followed him down, and the two of them brushed some dust and leaves from their clothes.

'I seem to be okay too,' I told them. 'I'm covered in scratches, bruises and grazes, but most of them seem to be from my **last** aeronautical escapade, not **this** one. Where's José?'

'Come over here and help me, my friends,' said José, right on cue. He was at the door of the helicopter, struggling with the latch. 'I do not wish to alarm you, but helicopters sometimes have a habit of exploding when they hit the ground. It is the fuel tanks, you understand. I think we should leave quickly.'

'Jolly good idea,' said Patrick the Magnificent. He clambered over the upturned seat and joined José at the door, and after a few hard pushes, it creaked open noisily, and the four of us clambered out and dropped to the ground.

We were surrounded by trees and bushes, some of which had broken branches where we had hit them during the crash landing. I turned around and looked at the twisted mass of metal.

'I guess we'll be getting home some other way,' I said.

'**Brilliant** deduction, Ocko,' said Spencer.

'This way,' said José, pushing branches aside and beating a path through the trees towards the open field.

We struggled along behind him, and after just a few seconds we emerged into the sunlight.

And there, standing in front of us like a row of soldiers on guard, were ten of the biggest, ugliest,

meanest big-headed rodents you could ever imagine seeing. **Tuco-tucos.**

The two tuco-tucos in the middle of the line suddenly jostled sideways to make room for someone else.

He stepped into the open field from behind them. Fat. White fur, and lots of it. Small, mean pink eyes.

A hush fell over the clearing. I found myself staring once more into the eyes of **Kurt Remarque**.

'Well, well, well,' he said slowly. 'Welcome to Nevado Mismi.'

16
THE TRUTH REVEALED — ALMOST

My nose was itchy. Really itchy. And when a rat's nose is itchy, it's a much more serious business than if **your** nose is itchy. After all, monkey people have ugly, tiny little noses that don't do anything except sit there, while we rats have huge, impressive snouts with whiskers — and when one of those huge impressive snouts starts to itch, you have a **real** problem.

So I had a **real** problem. What made it worse was that my arms were securely tied behind my back, so I couldn't scratch the itch. But even though my nose was so itchy that it was driving me crazy, I knew it wasn't my **biggest** problem.

No, my biggest problem was **much** bigger than that. My biggest problem was that I was being held captive by Kurt Remarque, the meanest and most ruthless criminal rat in the world, and by a gang of huge ugly tuco-tucos who looked as if they would like nothing better than to tear me snout from tail.

'You're **in big trouble, Kurt,'** I said.

There was a deep, ominous rumbling that made the ground shudder and the air vibrate. An earthquake? A tornado on the way? A plane flying low overhead?

Then I realised it was Kurt Remarque's idea of a laugh. It started as a low rumble in that huge stomach of his, and by the time it came out of his mouth it sounded like boulders falling over each other.

'You are **pathetic**, O'Malley, you know that?' he wheezed in between bouts of bellowing laughter. 'I'm in trouble? **I'm** in trouble? Think again, you moron. I think you'll find that **you're** the one in trouble here. You and your motley band of misfits and mice.'

He did have a point. I looked around the clearing. Spencer, Patrick and José were all tied up like me, and the tuco-tucos certainly looked as if they meant business.

I looked back at my old arch-enemy. It was time to play my trump card.

'You'll never get away with this, Kurt,' I said. 'I know exactly what you're up to, and I've notified the authorities.'

I'm not sure who looked more surprised — Kurt himself or my friends. I think Spencer was the winner. She looked at me as if I had gone completely crazy.

A flicker of doubt passed over Kurt's face and then he went back to his usual expression of smugness, but I knew I had rattled him.

'You have no idea what my plans **are**, you silly little policerat,' he bellowed. 'Your brain is too small to comprehend even **one tiny piece** of my scheme. Don't try and bluff me, Inspector.'

'It's not a bluff, Kurt,' I said steadily. 'And by the way, it's not **Inspector** either. I'm **Chief of Police** now, and don't you forget it.'

'I don't care if you're the **King of Ratworld**,' said Kurt. 'I still say you're too dumb to work out what day of the week it is, let alone my so-called **plan**.'

I took a deep breath. This was it. It was time to trust my instincts as the best police detective in the world. Time to fall back on my finely honed abilities and my truly brilliant mind. I took another breath, fixed him with my steeliest gaze, and began.

'It's **elementary**, my dear Kurt,' I began. 'You've faked your own death and secretly flown halfway around the world to the middle of Peru. You've invested your last dollar in a crazy scheme, gathering around you a band of tuco-tucos. Then you've travelled high up into the Andes to this little grassy knoll. **Why? Why** would you come all this way to this particular spot?'

I paused for dramatic effect.

Spencer was looking at me. Patrick was looking at me. José was looking at me. Kurt and all of the ugly tuco-tucos were looking at me. I was the centre of attention. They were hanging on my every word. Which is as it should be.

'Only a superb police mind like mine could piece together the clues in this mystery,' I said grandly. 'For anyone else, it would be too complicated, too far-fetched. But for Octavius O'Malley, it's just another day's work.'

'For goodness' sake, get on with it,' said Spencer. 'We're all **dying** to know.'

'Where are we?' I asked, ignoring her sarcastic outburst. 'We are in a very special place. This grassy knoll, with its little stream of water, is the source of the Amazon, the mightiest river in the world. Yes, that's right, Kurt, you didn't realise we knew that, did you? Well, I'll tell you something **else** I've worked out. You came here, with your band of tuco-tucos, **to destroy it!**'

Kurt stared at me blankly.

'What **on earth** are you talking about?' he said dumbly.

'Don't play dumb with me, Kurt,' I said. 'You think I don't know that the tuco-tucos are the best digging rodents in the world? You think I can't work out what your evil plan is? You're going to dig a new underground tunnel and make all the water flow off somewhere else. You're going to ruin the biggest and most important river in the world — the mighty Amazon, which waters half the crops in the world, helps the rainforests grow, and even supplies much of the air that we breathe, held to ransom by an evil rat! How could you do it, Kurt? **HOW?**'

I was silent, and everything was silent around me. I wasn't sure whether Spencer, José and Patrick had worked out Kurt's evil plan like I had, but I must say they all looked surprised. They sat there, eyes wide. The tuco-tucos were very quiet too. The air was still, and all you could hear was the low buzz of a passing insect.

Kurt slowly screwed up his nose and closed his eyes. His mouth opened wide and his head tilted back towards the sky. He looked as if he were about to bellow in rage, and I prepared myself for the onslaught. What would he do, now that his plan had been exposed?

And then it came — a slow, deep rumble like a landslide somewhere in the distance. It grew louder and louder, until it sounded like giant boulders.

Wait a minute.

Kurt was laughing.

LAUGHING! Deep gales of laughter, bouncing off the walls of the valley and echoing back until the whole place was filled with the sound.

One by one the tuco-tucos began to laugh too, a kind of ugly snorting laugh that almost sounded as if they were choking.

WHY was everybody laughing?

Kurt's rumbling laugh slowed a little, and he stared down at me.

'You really are a **dolt**, O'Malley,' he said, struggling for breath and holding his sides. 'The **Amazon**! What on earth would I want with the **Amazon**? How big a fool do you think I am?'

'Don't try and get out of this one, Remarque,' I said. 'Once you have closed off the source of the Amazon, you'll be able to demand a pretty price to restore it.'

Kurt was still laughing almost as hard.

'O'Malley, you are **too much!**' he said. 'I can't believe you're that stupid. Didn't you study any geography in that police school of yours, or science?'

'What do you mean?' I asked. I didn't like the way this conversation was going.

'Look, you fool,' went on Kurt, 'let's assume for a moment that your ridiculous idea is right. So I go and hire myself a bunch of tuco-tucos, dig a huge underground channel, and send the source of the Amazon flowing off towards the wrong sea. So what? Do you have any idea how many other rivers flow into the Amazon? Do you think it would make the slightest bit of difference if I stopped this miserable little drizzle here?'

'I think he's right my friends,' said José. 'There's the Apurimac River, and the Ucayali and the Maranon —'

'This is no time for a geography lesson, José,' I said angrily. 'I get the point.'

Kurt shuffled closer to me, until all I could see was a wall of white fur and two tiny pink eyes. He leant in until our snouts were almost touching, and whispered in a low, soft voice. 'I'll tell you what it's time for, O'Malley,' he hissed. 'It's time to get rid of you once and for all. You and your **pathetic** friends. When will you realise that it's not **about** evil plots or dastardly plans? It's not **about** rivers or ransom demands or revenge. It's about **money**. Pure and simple. **Money.** You took all my money once, and you thought you'd destroyed me. **BUT NO!!'**

He yelled the last two words so loudly my ears rang, then he began striding around the grassy knoll, bellowing so that all could hear.

'You destroyed my past in Rodent City, but you won't destroy my future! I died the day I left that city. I left my old name and my old reputation — the one that you destroyed — lying in the Rodent City graveyard. But here in these hills ... lies the one thing that will make me great again!'

'Water?' I said weakly. I still thought my theory was pretty good.

'No, you **IDIOT!**' bellowed Kurt. '**MONEY! Gold**, to be precise. More gold than your pathetic brain could ever imagine. The gold of the Incas, buried for hundreds of years. None of those stupid monkey people have ever been able to find it, but *they* know. *They* know.' As he spoke, Kurt was waving in the direction of the crowds of tuco-tucos.

'A treasure trove of gold, a king's ransom, hidden away for centuries. Hidden so well that it could never be found — at least, never found by a human. But one day a tuco-tuco was digging a tunnel, not far from where we are standing right now. The tunnel was long and deep, and suddenly this tuco-tuco came across a cave. A golden cave, a cave of unsurpassed riches.'

'The ransom of Atahualpa!'

I looked around at José, for it was he who had spoken.

'I have heard tales of these riches, my friend,' said José. 'Seven hundred thousand pieces of gold, gathered as a ransom for the great King Atahualpa, but never paid. Instead, it was hidden somewhere in a cave in the Andes, or so the legend goes.'

'This is no **legend**, you fool!' yelled Kurt. 'This is **the truth**. The tuco-tucos know where it is, they are just too stupid to work out what to do with it!'

The tuco-tucos didn't seem at all annoyed when Kurt called them stupid. They just stood there, watching. Maybe they really **were** stupid.

And then an idea suddenly tickled the back of my brain. What was it? What was I remembering?

Rodent City. Kurt's dessert stand, and the last day Kurt was seen there. Kurt had been talking to an ugly, big-headed rat . . .

'The ugly rat!' I blurted out.

'What?' said Kurt Remarque.

'That day in Rodent City, at your dessert stand. A witness saw you talking to an ugly rat with a huge head. That was a tuco-tuco, wasn't it?'

Kurt nodded thoughtfully.

'Yes,' he said. 'You may be stupid, but you **are** observant, I'll give you that. You just keep plodding away, gathering facts that you don't know what to do with. It **was** a tuco-tuco, a stowaway on a plane full of bananas who wound up in Rodent City. I took pity on him and gave him some food, and in return he told me his story — the story of a golden cave. I decided that very day that I would come here, hire a band of tuco-tucos, and make my fortune.'

He swept his pudgy white arm in a circle around the clearing.

'And so here we all are, and tomorrow my band of thick-headed helpers will lead me straight to the gold. Once I have it, nothing can stop me. A new fortune, a new identity and a new city where no one will ask **any** annoying questions.'

He came back to me again, until our snouts were almost touching once more, and I could smell his rank, fatty breath.

Especially not you, O'Malley. Once I have the gold, I'll be getting rid of you and your pesky friends for good. You escaped last time — you won't escape again. **TAKE THEM AWAY!**

The tuco-tucos grabbed us and bundled us down a track through some trees. We saw a mound of dirt sitting next to a hole. It was the entrance to a sort of deep pit that the tuco-tucos must have dug.

One by one we were pushed down into the hole, tumbling onto each other in the semi-darkness. A big mat of tangled tree branches was dragged across the entrance, and two of the biggest, ugliest tuco-tucos were left as guards.

Spencer looked at me.

'Don't say a word,' I said.

17
THE GOLD OF ATAHUALPA

'The gold of Atahualpa?' I said. 'Can it possibly be true?'

'Yes indeed, my friends,' said José. 'I heard this story many times when I was little.'

'The lost treasure of the Incas, Ocko,' said Spencer. 'I've heard that story too. I thought it was just a myth.'

'Me too,' said Patrick. 'It was a ransom meant to be paid to the Spanish, but after the great Incan leader died, it was hidden away instead, and never found again.'

It seemed everyone had heard the story except me. I guess I'd been reading the wrong kinds of books.

'Okay, so it's true,' I said. 'What do we do now? We're stuck here, tied up in a hole in the ground, being guarded by two enormous tuco-tucos with the combined IQ of a twig.'

'Good question,' said Spencer. 'I don't suppose you have a **plan**?'

I sighed. 'Of course,' I said. 'You always want a plan.

Well here's a plan. It's very straightforward. We break out of this hole, find the cave with the buried gold, thwart Kurt Remarque's evil plan, arrest him, take him back to Rodent City, prove that he faked his death as part of an international conspiracy to rob the good people of Lima of their hidden gold, and put him in gaol for a very long time. Then we have lunch, because I'm starving.'

'Sounds **perfect**!' said Patrick. 'So how do we manage all that?'

'That's the hard part,' I said. 'I haven't a clue.'

It is a very difficult thing for a brilliant policerat like me to admit when I'm out of ideas, but sometimes there's no other choice.

'If we could at least get these ropes undone,' said Spencer. 'Come on, Patrick, you're meant to be able to open any door and pick any lock. Can't you do something with these ropes?'

'Not without a toothpick,' said Patrick glumly. 'It's **hopeless**.'

'Ah, there is always hope, my friends,' said José.

'Really?' I said excitedly. 'You have a **plan**? A way out of here?'

'Of course not,' said José cheerfully. 'I am just saying that there is always hope.'

'Great, I'll try to remember that,' I said, settling back down on the floor. This really **is hopeless**, I thought to myself.

I was hungry, thirsty and miserable. I thought of my cosy little office back in Rodent City. It was the middle of the morning, and right about now, Deputy Smith would be bringing me a nice cup of coffee and a doughnut. Maybe it would be a chocolate doughnut with jam in the middle, or a pineapple doughnut, or a pink one with sprinkles all over it . . .

As I lay there daydreaming, I heard a commotion above us. It sounded like more tuco-tucos had arrived at the entrance to the hole. I could hear a lot of chattering and a few sounds of **tuco-tuco, tuco-tuco** as they spoke to the guards. And then all of a sudden the mat of tree branches was dragged away and sunlight poured in, making me shut my eyes.

When I opened them again I was staring up at four huge ugly heads.

'This is not good,' said Spencer.

'Not good at all,' I agreed.

'Do you think they've come to kill us?' said Patrick.

'Very likely, I think,' said José.

'Hey!' I said. 'You were supposed to be the **optimistic** one, remember? "There is always hope?"'

'Of course,' went on José, 'but sometimes you must be realistic, my friends.'

There was movement from above, and one of the tuco-tucos dropped down into the hole with us. He immediately reached for Spencer.

'Hey! Leave her alone!' I said, struggling to my feet.

184

The tuco-tuco immediately left Spencer alone, and reached for me instead.

'Um, on second thoughts …' I added, but it was too late. He had me firmly in his grasp.

'Tell them I died bravely,' I said, even though I wasn't feeling the least bit brave.

The tuco-tuco tightened his grip around me, took a deep breath, grunted, and threw me up into the air. I flew straight through the opening above and landed on the grass, where I was immediately surrounded by the three other tuco-tucos. Not a wonderful situation to be in, you understand, but at least I wasn't dead.

There was a sort of **WHOSH**ing sound and I felt a rush of air, then suddenly Spencer landed right on top of me. Luckily she is relatively small — that is one good thing about mice. She hit me right in the stomach and then bounced off onto the ground.

'**OOOFF!** Sorry, Ocko,' she said. 'I didn't really get the chance to aim.'

'No problem,' I muttered, rubbing my stomach. 'At least I broke your fall.'

'So what's going on? Do you think — **OOOFF!**' said Spencer, as there was another rush of air and Patrick landed right on top of **her**.

'Sorry,' said Patrick. 'I couldn't —'

'Hang on, hang on!' I interrupted.

'**What?**' said Patrick and Spencer together.

'I've just realised what's coming next! **MOVE!**'

We tried to scramble back out of the way just as there came another **WHOOSH**ing sound. There was a flash of multicoloured poncho and a **THUD**, and José landed in a heap right in the middle of us.

He didn't even have time to catch his breath before the tuco-tucos began pushing us across the grass to where a narrow pathway disappeared through the trees.

'Caminen!' grunted the tuco-tuco who was directly behind me, and he shoved me in the back.

'It means **walk**,' said José helpfully, but I didn't really need a translator for that. The tuco-tuco shoved me again, so I walked.

We stumbled along the narrow track through thick jungle until suddenly it opened up into another clearing. This one had a road winding through it, just wide enough for a large car or a truck to travel along. There was a huge rusty container, like the kind you see on wharves, sitting by the side of the road. It had big black letters stencilled on the side — **PKFNW** — and the number **8**. The tuco-tucos led us straight past it.

Behind the container, hidden from the road, was a small pile of dirt and a hole. A tuco-tuco hole. Sitting next to the hole on a folding chair, with a cool glass of iced tea in his fat white hand, was Kurt Remarque.

'How **lovely** to see you again,' he said, sipping from his frosty glass.

There was a scrabbling sound from inside the hole

and then a tuco-tuco popped his head out. His body soon followed, and resting on his back was a small carved box about the size of this book you are reading. A golden box, shining in the sunlight.

The tuco-tuco scurried over to the big shipping container, opened the door at the back, and heaved the golden box inside. It clanged against something else that was already in there. Then the tuco-tuco disappeared back down the hole.

'Now, we have a slight problem,' Kurt continued. 'There is a truck arriving here in just a few hours to collect this rather large container and deliver it to its new home — **my** new home.'

'You'll never get away with this,' I said for no particular reason. In actual fact, I couldn't really think of one good reason why he **wouldn't** get away with it.

'Stop being so **tiresome**, O'Malley,' said Kurt Remarque. **'Of course** I'll get away with it. But you see I have slightly miscalculated the amount of time I will need to load all this gold.'

Kurt pushed himself up from his seat, placed his iced tea carefully on the ground, and waddled over to where we were standing.

'Personally, O'Malley, I blame **you**,' he said. 'If I hadn't wasted all that valuable time capturing you and your foolish friends, I wouldn't be running late now. So I am prepared to make you an offer.'

He pulled a small knife out of one of his pockets.

'I will free you and your friends and you will go with the tuco-tucos and help them carry the gold. We need all hands on deck, so to speak.'

'And what's in it for us?' I said.

'I won't kill you ... **yet**,' said Kurt Remarque ominously, smiling the kind of smile that makes your blood run cold. At least, it certainly made **my** blood run cold.

'Boy, with an offer like that, how could we refuse?' said Patrick. I think he was being sarcastic, but he was right anyway. What else could we do?

Kurt cut our ropes and then went back to his seat in the shade of a convenient tree. He picked up his iced tea, took a sip, then stretched himself out in his chair.

'Off you go, then,' he said. 'And remember, for every piece of gold you carry, I'll let you live another minute. Ha!'

Lovely rat, that Kurt Remarque.

The tuco-tucos pushed us down the hole and stayed close behind us as we scuttled along the dark, damp tunnel through the earth. There were still tuco-tucos coming back the other way, loaded down with gold. Some were carrying golden vases on their backs; others had bowls or piles of thick golden chains. There was just enough room for them to squeeze past us.

Soon enough, the tunnel widened out, turned a corner, then opened into a huge cave. The tuco-tucos had put candles in each corner, and their weak spluttering flames lit up a huge pile of treasure.

There were hundreds — no, **thousands** — of objects made of solid gold. Statues, goblets, thick golden bands designed to be worn like crowns, huge plates the size of pizzas, and great piles of thick chains. On the wall of the cavern, behind the gold, was a huge stone head with carved eyes and nose, and a big toothy smile. It looked as if it were staring down on the treasure, protecting it.

'**Wow!**' said Patrick.

'**Unbelievable,**' said Spencer.

'Muevete!' said one of the tuco-tucos closest to me, shoving me rudely in the back.

'That means —' said José, but I interrupted him.

'Don't worry about the translation, José,' I muttered. 'I think I can work it out myself.'

I went over to the nearest pile of gold vases and lifted one onto my shoulders. It was heavy. It was so heavy that, when it was their turn, Spencer and Patrick had to carry one between them, each holding one end.

We joined the queue of tuco-tucos shuffling up and down the tunnel, from the cave to the container and back again. It was hard work, made even harder by the fact that we were working for Kurt Remarque. I never thought I would see the day when a brilliant policerat like me

would be reduced to working for an evil master-criminal.

So much for my great police work. So much for my dazzling investigations, and my cunning plans and my **huge** brain.

We went back and forth at least a dozen times, until my back was aching and my legs were weak and wobbly. Finally, there were no more than half a dozen gold plates and a small pile of jewels left in the cave.

I was about to haul one of the last of the plates onto my shoulders when I heard a groan from behind me and turned to see a body slump to the ground. It was José, and he was moaning softly.

I rushed over.

'José, José, what's wrong?' I whispered as I knelt down beside him. He kept moaning and holding his back, and then he looked into my eyes ... and winked.

Just then, Spencer and Patrick came out of the tunnel into the cave, ready for their next load. They hurried over to join me.

'Is he okay?' said Spencer anxiously.

There were three tuco-tucos in the cavern, watching us impatiently.

'Que pasa?' said one of them gruffly.

'I don't understand Spanish!' I said angrily. 'My friend is sick.'

'They want to know what is happening,' whispered José between his moans. 'Just say Mi amigo se muere. It means **My friend is dying**.'

'Mi amigo se muere,' I said.

The tuco-tucos started muttering to themselves. They knew there were only a few more loads of gold to carry and that the truck would be coming soon.

One of them came over to us and José moaned, rolled his eyes and coughed, sending them scurrying away again. Finally, they each grabbed a golden plate, hauled it onto their backs and disappeared back up the tunnel.

The four of us were alone in the cave.

José jumped to his feet. It was the fastest recovery I had ever seen.

'Quickly, my friends,' he said, 'we only have a few seconds. Follow me.'

'But the only exit is the tunnel,' I said. 'We'll run straight into the tuco-tucos.'

'Not if we go this way!' said José.

He raced to the back of the cavern, to the wall where the gold had been stacked. He reached up and wrapped both of his arms around the huge carved head on the wall.

'Right,' he said, 'everybody pull, **now!**'

José put both of his legs against the wall, held tightly on to the carved head, and pulled. I wrapped my arms around José and pulled too. Spencer grabbed my tail, and Patrick grabbed her tail, and we all pulled like in a tug-of-war.

There was a creaking sound, and a groaning sound, and a **POP** like a cork coming out of a bottle, and suddenly we were tumbling backwards over each other. The huge carved head had burst out of its place on the wall, revealing a narrow space behind it just wide enough to crawl through. Light was filtering through the hole from somewhere up above.

'Quick, my friends,' said José, 'we haven't a moment to lose. **Go! Through the hole!**'

I gave Patrick a boost up and he disappeared into the gap in the wall. Spencer followed and I went after her.

After a few seconds, I stopped and looked around. Where was José?

I turned awkwardly and crawled back to the cavern. José was half in the hole and half out of it, with his back to me. He was leaning back into the cavern to grab the carved head with both hands.

'You must pull hard on my tail,' he said when he heard me behind him. 'I can hear the tuco-tucos coming.'

I grabbed his tail and began crawling back up the tunnel, dragging José and the carved head behind me. José jammed the head back into place, closing off the hole again.

'Now they won't know where we have gone — at least for a while,' he said. 'Let's get out of here. Even a stupid tuco-tuco will work it out sooner or later . . .'

'But how did you know about the hole hidden behind the head?' I asked.

'I'll explain later, my friend', said José. 'Right now, I think we should keep moving, don't you?'

'Excellent plan,' I said.

We crawled through the tunnel and soon caught up with Spencer and Patrick. Minutes later it ended in an overgrown clump of bushes on the side of a hill.

We were free.

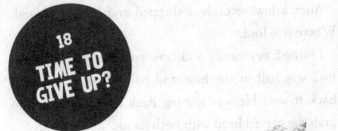

18
TIME TO GIVE UP?

'More coffee, my friends?' said José, shuffling over to the little stove at the back of his comfortable room.

I was just finishing off my third extra-sugary doughnut, and a coffee would be the perfect accompaniment.

'Great idea,' I said.

'Me too,' said Spencer.

'I'm fine,' said Patrick, who was not a big fan of coffee.

I lay back on the hessian sacks that José kept scattered around his room, and stretched. I had slept well, eaten well, and I was feeling great. My fur had even started to grow back.

It was hard to believe that just yesterday we had been captured by Kurt Remarque and certain death had seemed the only thing we had to look forward to. Then, as if by magic, José had hauled down that huge stone head, led us through an escape tunnel to the other side of the mountain, and we were free. We'd scuttled down to the roadway and walked until we came across a truck that had stopped by the side of the road while the driver visited a local café.

As far as trucks go, it was an extremely comfortable one, carrying a load of blankets destined for the shops of Lima. It took us all the way back to José's room, where we were all so exhausted we just grabbed the nearest sack and slept.

And now here we were, gorging on doughnuts and coffee. **Does life get any better?**

'Tell me about that carved head,' I said to José. 'I still can't work out how you knew it was disguising a way out.'

'It's very simple, my friend,' said José as he poured steaming coffee into a mug. 'I told you I come from a village in the valley of the Incas. I saw many of these carved heads. Keystones, they call them. The Incas would carve a head to act as a good spirit, to watch over their families and their villages.'

'Yes, but so what?' said Spencer. 'How did you know there would be an escape tunnel behind it?'

'Well, think about it,' said José. 'The tunnel that the tuco-tucos used to come into the cave was one **they** had dug **themselves**. So there **must** have been another way out — the way the Incas used when they put the gold there hundreds of years ago.'

'**Ye-e-es**,' I said slowly, 'but how did you know that tunnel was behind the stone head?'

'I didn't, really,' confessed José, 'but I figured that the stone head was the last thing they put in place before they closed up the cave with all the gold inside, so if it were me, I would have used the head to close up the cave and help hide it.'

'And that's exactly what they did!' exclaimed Patrick. '**Brilliant!**'

'History is a wonderful thing, my friends,' said José, settling down beside us with his coffee and passing mugs to Spencer and me. 'The past has many things to teach us.'

'Maybe,' I said, 'but it's the future I'm worried about right now. **Kurt Remarque's** future.'

'Perhaps you should just let him go,' said Spencer. 'The gold is gone, but what harm has been done? It has been sitting forgotten in that cave for hundreds of years. It is no one's gold now, and no one will miss it.'

'That may be true,' I said, 'but what worries me is what Kurt Remarque will **do** with all his new millions. No matter how much money he has, that rat always wants more. As long as he stays poor, he can't cause much trouble. But once he is rich again, there will be **no end** to his evil plots.'

'Maybe so,' went on Spencer, 'but we can't just chase him around the world forever.'

'Yeah,' added Patrick. 'Besides, we don't even know where he was going. He could be **anywhere** by now.'

'What do **you** think, José?'

I turned to face our Peruvian friend. He had been very quiet during this conversation, sitting and sipping his coffee thoughtfully.

'Hmm?' he said, looking up from his steaming cup. 'I'm sorry, my friend, I wasn't listening. I was miles away.'

'Thinking about the treasure, I'll bet,' said Patrick.

'Thinking about a **different** treasure,' said José. 'I was thinking about all those years ago, when the men came to my village and took away everything, even the vase I was in. I think perhaps strangers have **always** come to Peru to take away our treasures. First the humans, and now this Kurt Remarque.'

'So what do you think we should do?' I asked. 'Should we chase after him, or not?'

'I cannot make that decision for you, my friend,' said José. 'I just feel sad for my country. **Always** people come here to steal.'

José went back to sipping his coffee. I looked at him, and tried to imagine him as a young rat, far away from his family and home, wondering if anyone would help him.

Spencer looked and caught my eye. I raised an eyebrow. She raised one back at me. I looked over at Patrick. He winked.

'That's it,' I said. 'I've made up my mind. We're going after him.'

'**That's** the spirit,' said Spencer. 'What have we got to lose, except more fur?'

'Okay, so how do we find out where Kurt Remarque is now?' said Patrick.

'A good question,' said José. 'Peru is a big country. South America is even bigger. He could be **anywhere**.'

'Anywhere at all,' said Patrick sadly. 'We could spend the rest of our lives looking for him. And don't forget, as far as Rodent City is concerned, he's dead. I'm sure the Mayor won't want to see their Chief of Police spending all his time looking for a dead man.'

'Wait a minute!' said Spencer. '**I know where he is!**'

'You **do**?' I asked, surprised.

'Sure,' said Spencer. 'How heavy is gold?'

'What?' I asked.

'You heard me,' said Spencer with growing excitement.

'How heavy is gold?'

'It's **very** heavy,' I said. 'You know that. You had to lug all those plates and vases around with Patrick, remember?'

'**Of course** I remember,' said Spencer. 'So it's heavy, right?'

'Yes, it's heavy,' I repeated, exasperated.

'Well, Kurt Remarque is now the proud owner of hundreds and hundreds of really heavy things, isn't he?'

'Do you have to remind me?'

'Yes I do,' said Spencer. 'Think about it, Ocko. He has all this gold in a huge container and he's got to get it back home — wherever **that** is. Now, he's not going to put it on a **plane**, is he?'

'I suppose not,' I said slowly. 'It would be much too

heavy to carry on a plane, I guess. Or you'd need a really big one, and that would attract too much attention.'

'So it has to be a **ship**!' said Spencer triumphantly.

'Yes, but **which** ship?' said Patrick.

'I don't know,' said Spencer, 'but how many ships could there possibly be in the Lima port that would be big enough to carry a container full of gold?'

I jumped to my feet. 'I don't know,' I said, 'but there can't be **that** many. I think we should go straight down to the wharves and find out.'

Spencer jumped up too.

'Now **that**,' she said, 'is a **plan**.'

****

Rats love ports. All those ships being loaded and unloaded, trucks full of every kind of food and drink — it's **paradise**. There are warehouses stacked full of meat, vegetables and fruit, waiting to be delivered. And for every warehouse there is a network of ratruns and passageways where the local rats can carry off their share. The port of Lima — Callao, it is called — was familiar ground to José.

'I come here every week,' said José, 'sometimes twice a week.'

We had travelled along a drain that passed under the main highway to the port, then slipped up a drainpipe and across the huge rooftops of the warehouses, then down again via a space between two walls, finally coming out through a small grate.

We found ourselves on the waterfront. There were forklifts darting back and forth, carrying piles of boxes. Men were everywhere, shouting and calling out to each other and generally getting in the way. Typical monkey people, really. And high over our heads were huge cranes, lifting giant shipping containers and moving them around as if they were no more than matchboxes.

All of that was exciting, but I was more interested in seeing how many ships were in the dock. There were three. Two huge grey ones, their decks stacked with containers, and a smaller ship at the very end of the dock that looked empty and forgotten.

'**Whew!**' said Patrick. 'Where do we start?'

'I guess we just have to spread out and check every ship,' I said. 'Can anyone remember what Kurt Remarque's container looked like?'

'It was old,' said Spencer. 'Old and rusty. That's about all I can remember.'

'It had some letters and a number on it,' said Patrick. 'I'm sure one of the letters was **P**, and I *know* the number was **8** because that's my lucky number.'

'Good work, Patrick the Magnificent,' I said. 'That will help narrow things down. So let's spread out and look for a rusty old container with a **P** and an **8** on it.

The first one to find it, just whistle three times and the rest of us will come running.'

'Wait a minute, my friends,' said José. He pointed at the first ship.

The crane had swung over until it was right on top of the ship. It lowered down, latched onto one of the containers on board and slowly lifted it into the air and swung it back towards the dock.

'What about it?' I asked.

'You see?' said José. 'It is **un**loading, not loading. The crane is taking containers **off** the ship. I think this means our gold will not be there. We need a ship that is taking **on** containers, not taking them **off**.'

'Good point,' I said. 'Forget the first ship. Patrick, you and José start with the big ship next to it. Spencer and I will quickly check out the old one and then come back and join you.'

We headed down the wharf, staying in the shadows of the buildings whenever we could to avoid attracting too much attention from the monkey people.

Patrick and José hitched a ride on the back of a passing forklift that was heading for the big ship, while Spencer and I kept walking towards the smaller old one at the end of the wharf.

'I'm not even sure that ship's big enough to carry a container,' said Spencer when we got closer. 'It looks pretty sad.'

Spencer was right. It was seemed pretty broken-down. The paint was dull and patchy and you could see that some of the windows along the side were cracked.

'I think we could be wasting our time,' I said.

'Oh, well,' said Spencer, 'the sooner we give it the quick once-over, the sooner we can get back to the other two.'

Right at that moment a truck came hurtling down the wharf, almost bowling us over.

'Hey! What's the big idea?' I yelled, shaking my fist at the truck that was rattling away in a cloud of grey smoke. 'You could have —'

And then I stopped, and grabbed Spencer's arm.

The truck had a large container on the back of it. A rusty old container, with letters and numbers written on the side. As the smoke cleared a little, I squinted so that I could just make them out.

'P ... K ... F ... N ... W ...' I recited to Spencer. 'And what's that last one at the end? Is it a "B"?'

'No,' said Spencer, moving quickly down the wharf after the truck, 'it's an **8. That's our gold!**'

I let out three loud whistles and looked around. I couldn't see Patrick and José anywhere. I glanced back and Spencer was already halfway down the wharf. I whistled once more and then I followed.

I caught up to Spencer at the end of the wharf. She was hiding behind a rubbish bin directly opposite the old wooden boat.

'Look,' she said.

The truck had stopped and was slowly and carefully driving backwards up a couple of wooden planks that led directly onto the old ship. It was a dangerous manoeuvre — one mistake and the truck would have gone tumbling into the water.

Eventually the truck made it all the way to the top of the planks, its back wheels just touching the deck of the old ship. There was a low whining sound like an electric drill, and slowly the whole back of the truck began to tip up into the air. The container slowly slid off the back of the truck and disappeared through an opening on the deck of the ship into the hold below. There was a loud **THUD**, a **CRACK** and a cloud of dust, then all was quiet.

'What do we do now?' said Spencer.

'I don't know,' I said. 'Do you think there are any laws against removing Incan treasure from Peru?'

'Beats me,' said Spencer. '**You're** the policerat.'

'The other big question,' I went on, 'is where on earth is Kurt Remarque?'

No sooner had the words left my mouth than there was a firm tap on my shoulder from behind. I jumped two metres in the air — and turned around to see José and Patrick.

'**Don't do that!**' I yelled. 'You just took five years off my life!'

'Sorry,' said José, 'did we scare you?'

'No, no,' I said, 'I don't scare **that** easily. I was just — just — caught by surprise, that's all.'

'So why did you whistle before?' said Patrick. 'We heard it and then it took us ages to find you. Why are you hiding behind this rubbish bin?'

'**The gold is on that ship,**' said Spencer, pointing to the old vessel at the wharf. 'We saw the container being loaded.'

'All that heavy gold on that rotten old ship?' said Patrick. 'Are you **sure**?'

'No doubt about it,' I put in. 'The same rusty container, and the code on the side was **PKFNW8**.'

'That sounds like it, my friends,' said José. 'What now?'

At that moment there was a huge blast of noise, and a belch of smoke burst from the funnel of the old ship. There was another blast from the foghorn, and the old ship shuddered and shook at the dock. I noticed men running towards it, and one of them reached down to untie a huge rope.

'**It's leaving!**' I said. 'There's no time to waste. We need to get on board.'

'Why? What are we going to do?' said Spencer.

'Yes, what's the **plan**?' said Patrick.

Of course I had absolutely no idea.

'I'll tell you later,' I said. 'Quick, follow me before they cast off the last rope.'

There were four huge ropes running from the ship to the dock, and one of them had already been cast off. A couple of men were working on the second one, and even as we raced across the wharf it came loose and was tossed aside. The men headed for the third rope. **We** headed for the fourth.

The third rope was cast off just as we started climbing up the fourth one. I led the way, with José following close behind and the two mice behind him. We had made it halfway up the rope by the time the men arrived at the bottom to release it.

Then we hit a slight problem.

There was a large metal plate attached to the rope.

It was like a giant pizza tray and the rope was threaded straight through the middle of it. I knew immediately what it was — it was a barrier that the monkey people put there to stop rats from running up the rope and getting onto the ship. As if **that** would stop an enterprising rat like me!

I jumped up in the air, grabbed the edge of the metal plate and did an elegant backflip so that I could sail gracefully over it and land on the rope on the other side. It worked perfectly right up to the moment when I caught my left leg on the edge of the plate, bounced face-first off the rope, sailed into the air again and this time missed the rope and started plummeting towards the water below. **Yikes!**

Just as I was preparing myself for disaster, I was snapped back into the air again. José had me by the tail. He flicked me into the air and I landed safely back on the rope — on the right side of the metal disc, too.

I quickly helped José to clamber over, and Spencer and Patrick followed. I looked down to see the men untying the end of our rope and tossing it to the ground.

'Go, go, go!' I said. We raced up the rope just as it went all loose and floppy below us. With seconds to spare, we shot through the small hole in the bow of the ship where the rope was connected, slithered down the side of the hold, and landed on a huge pile of sacks with **FINEST PERUVIAN WHEAT** stamped on them. The ship shuddered, groaned, squeaked and rattled, and began to move slowly from the dock.

I looked up, and there in the middle of the hold was the rusty container. **But WHERE was Kurt?**

'Tricky,' I said thoughtfully.

'**Very** tricky,' said Spencer.

When you are a very experienced policerat, as I am, there are many things you have to put up with. Chasing dangerous criminals. **Being chased** by dangerous criminals. Searching for things that have been stolen. Investigating clues. But this was very unusual.

'So, just to recap,' I said, 'we're stuck on a creaky old boat with the lost treasure of the Incas, heading out into the Pacific Ocean ...'

'With no idea where we're going,' added Patrick.

'And no idea where the evil mastermind Kurt Remarque is,' put in Spencer.

'So now what?' I finished.

'I think it is simple,' said José. He was still leaning back on the sacks of wheat, looking like a rat without a care in the world.

'We have a famous saying in Peru,' said José. '**The**

llama will go to the mountains.'

He looked at us expectantly.

'Ye–es,' said Spencer slowly. 'So what exactly does that mean?'

'Isn't it obvious, my friends?' said José. **The llama will go to the mountains.** Or to put it another way, **the tuco–tuco will find his hole. The condor will soar to the clouds. The dog will sleep in the sun.**'

'What **on earth** are you talking about?' I said.

José sighed. 'I mean that all things can be found where they need to be. The llama loves the mountains, so that is where he will go. Tuco-tucos love to dig, the condor loves to fly high in the sky, the dog —'

'Okay, okay,' I said. 'I think I've got the general idea. But why are you telling us this **now**?'

'Well,' said José patiently, 'we have found the gold, yes, but we have not found Kurt. This is bad.'

'I agree,' I said.

'So we must find him, but where should we look?'

'He could be **anywhere**,' said Spencer. 'He could be in a plane somewhere, flying to wherever this boat is heading, so that he is ready and waiting when his gold arrives.'

'Yes, he could be,' said José, 'but I do not think that he is. Remember, all things can be found where they need to be. I don't believe Kurt would let his gold out of his sight. **I think he is right here on this boat.**'

'But **where?**' said Patrick.

'Well, if José is right,' I said, 'we can either wait for Kurt to find **us**, or we can go out and find **him**.'

'Search the boat?' said Spencer.

'Exactly,' I replied.

And so we did.

It was a small ship, so it didn't really take too long. The hold had barely enough room for the huge container. Apart from the sacks of Peruvian wheat we had landed on, there were a few crates of vegetables, half a dozen long coiled ropes, and six big barrels with the word **WHISKY** stamped on the side.

'He could be hiding in one of the barrels,' said Patrick.

'Well if he is, he's going to be pretty drunk,' said Spencer.

'And he'd have to be able to hold his breath for an awfully long time too,' I added. 'I don't see any air holes.'

'Oh yeah,' said Patrick. 'Dumb idea, I guess.'

Typical for a mouse, I thought, but I didn't say it. No need to be nasty, after all.

'He's obviously not down here,' said Spencer. 'Do you think it's safe to check up on deck?'

'Only one way to find out,' I said. 'Let's go.'

I climbed up the creaky wooden ladder that led through the open hatch and onto the deck. As soon as I got close, I slowed down and sniffed the air. Salt water and fish were all I could smell — no monkey people close by. There was a breeze blowing in from the ocean, and every now and then a seagull would come screeching overhead, hovering on the currents of air and then floating away again.

'Okay, let's get this over with,' I said. 'As soon as we get up there, we'll spread out. I'll go forward to the bridge; Spencer, you go to the left side of the boat, Patrick to the right. José, you check up the back. If you see a human, keep quiet, but if you see Kurt, make as much noise as you can and we'll all come running. Agreed?'

I looked down the ladder at the others crouching below me. All three nodded.

We scrambled onto the deck and went off in our different directions, looking for little nooks and crannies where we could hide from sight. As it turned out, that wasn't really necessary.

There were only three sailors on the deck, all of them asleep. It must have been hard work getting the boat ready to sail, because they were resting against a little upturned rowboat, snoring like walruses.

I headed towards the front of the ship, where there was a small cabin with cracked and smudged windows. This was where the captain would be, steering the ship. It was dangerous, but I had to look inside. I couldn't imagine why Kurt would be in there, but you never knew.

I climbed on top of some empty boxes and tried looking in through the window, but it was too dirty; I couldn't see a thing. I jumped down and moved around to the door. I put my ear against the old, rotten wood, and listened.

Over the howling of the wind, the screeching of seagulls and the slap of the water below, I heard a deep, rumbling noise like rocks bumping up against each other. I couldn't believe it! **Kurt Remarque's laugh!** I'd know that sound anywhere.

I took two steps back and launched myself against the door.

There was a **CRACK** of splitting wood, the rotten, mouldy door broke and I found myself tumbling head over tail into the narrow bridge of the ship.

I leapt to my feet, slipped over an old piece of rope, fell forward again, jumped up, knocked my head against a low shelf, slid sideways into the wall as the ship took a particularly large wave, fell over again, and finally staggered back to my feet and yelled, **'Kurt Remarque! You're under arrest!'**

I was staring straight into the eyes of the ship's captain. He was sitting on a rickety stool at the ship's wheel, steering a course across the ocean. He was old and ugly and unshaven, with three teeth missing and a gold ring through his ear. And he was alone. **Completely** alone. No Kurt Remarque to be seen.

I just had time to notice a large radio on the shelf next to him, blaring out some kind of distorted music with a loud, thumping beat like the sound of rocks bashing against each other. Then I saw an empty coffee mug sailing through the air in my direction.

'Lárgate, rata asquerosa!' yelled the captain,

L'ARGATE, RATA ASQUEROSA!

reaching for something else to throw. He grabbed a butter knife from the table in front of him, and I didn't wait around to see how good his aim was. I ran.

Five seconds later we were all back down in the hold, resting on the wheat sacks. I was still out of breath. I'm not as fit as I used to be.

'So much for **that** bright idea,' I puffed. 'No Kurt up there, no Kurt down here.'

'I don't understand,' said José. 'The llama will **always** go to the mountain.'

'Well that's great for the llama,' I said, 'but it doesn't help us.'

'You know, there is one other possibility,' said Spencer quietly. 'The gold might not be in this container after all.'

'Nonsense!' I said angrily. 'This is definitely the same container I saw up in the mountains.'

'That may be so,' said Spencer, 'but how do we know Kurt didn't take the gold out and put it somewhere else?'

I turned to Patrick.

'Well, what do **you** think, Patrick the Magnificent?' I asked. 'Do you reckon you can pick that lock?'

'Please!' said Patrick, sounding mightily offended. 'I could do it with my eyes closed!'

'Yes,' said Spencer, 'but can you do it on a broken-down, rocking boat in the middle of the Pacific Ocean with your eyes **open**, when you don't have your toothpick and chewing gum to help you?'

'Watch and learn,' said Patrick the Magnificent, jumping up from the sack. He walked slowly towards the locked door of the container, pausing along the way to prise a sharp, narrow splinter of wood from the rotting floor of the boat.

'Careful!' I said. 'That wooden floor is the only thing between us and the bottom of the ocean.'

'Relax,' said Patrick casually. 'One little splinter won't make a difference.'

The splinter had left a tiny crack. Patrick patted it gently with his foot and then sauntered over to the container. He reached into his waistcoat pocket and pulled out the oldest, furriest piece of chewing gum I'd ever seen. It looked like it had been chewed a hundred times.

'This has been chewed a hundred times, but it still works,' said Patrick.

The container doors were held together with a long metal bolt, and the bolt was secured by a padlock. Patrick stuck the old piece of gum into the keyhole of the padlock, pushed the splinter of wood straight through the middle of it, and began to slowly work it back and forth.

'It's ... **HHMMMPFF** ... a relatively simple ... **UUURGH** ... exercise, even without the ... **AAAHH** ... best-quality chewing gum to lubricate it all,' said Patrick, fiddling and pushing the lock as he spoke.

There was a loud click and the padlock jumped open. Patrick unhooked it with a flourish, drew back the bolt and threw open the double door at the back of the container, turning to face us as he did so.

'**Ta-da!**' he said triumphantly.

I looked over his shoulder into the container and, using my brilliant police skills, I immediately noticed three things.

First, the gold was indeed all there, stacked up and gleaming in the dim light of the hold.

Second, **Kurt Remarque** was there as well, leaning back comfortably in a deckchair placed next to the gold.

Third, and probably most important, **he had a gun pointing straight at us.**

'Just like a llama!' said José.

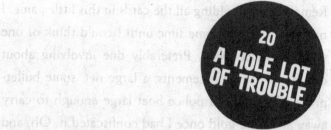

'You never **learn**, do you, O'Malley?' sneered Kurt Remarque, struggling to his feet and emerging from inside the container. 'You should have stayed in Peru — or better yet, you should never have left Rodent City.'

'What can I tell you, Kurt?' I replied. 'I always did enjoy a long sea journey.'

'Well, I'm afraid this is going to be a **short** sea journey for you and your friends,' said Kurt, his little pink eyes darting from me to Spencer, then to Patrick, before finally coming to rest on José. 'A **very** short journey, with a **very** nasty end.'

'What are you going to do, shoot us all?' said Spencer.

'If I have to,' said Kurt coldly. 'But I thought it might be better all round if you went for a swim instead.'

'But I can't swim,' blurted out Patrick.

'So much the better,' said Kurt.

This wasn't looking good. I could see that Kurt

Remarque was holding all the cards in this little game. I had to try to buy some time until I could think of one of my **brilliant plans**. Preferably one involving about one hundred reinforcements, a large net, some bullet-proof armour and a police boat large enough to carry away all of the gold once I had confiscated it. Oh, and a couple of dozen doughnuts, too. There is always a place for doughnuts in every brilliant plan.

Of course, right now I had none of those things. That's why I needed time.

'See that porthole over there?' said Kurt, gesturing to one side with his gun.

There was a round porthole about halfway up the side of the boat. The glass was dingy and dirty, crusted with the salt of a thousand journeys. It was held in place by a small rusty handle.

'Inspector — sorry, **Police Chief** — O'Malley,' said Kurt. 'If you would be so kind as to go over there and open it, I think you'll find it's just big enough for you all to fit through.'

This was it. I had to think fast. After all, there were four of us and only one of him. If we all rushed him at once, I was sure we could overpower him. But I had to find a way to signal to the others. Perhaps I could use some sort of code language.

'Yes, certainly Kurt,' I replied slowly. I glanced across at Spencer and Patrick, wriggling my eyebrows and staring deliberately at them. Then I went on very, very

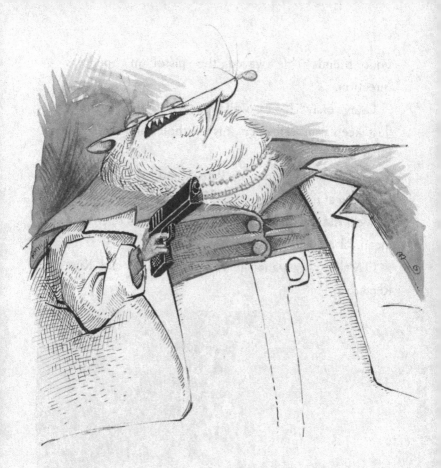

slowly. 'So what you are saying, Kurt, is that if I open the porthole we could ... **ALL ... RUSH ... YOU!**'

'What?' said Kurt, his eyes narrowing until they were just slits in his fat white face. 'What are you talking about?'

'I said we could **all rush through**,' I said quickly. 'If I open the porthole, we could **all rush through**.'

'You can go as fast as you like,' said Kurt impatiently. 'The sooner you are out of here, the better. Now, get that porthole open, O'Malley, before I shoot one of your friends.' He waved the pistol in Spencer's direction.

'Okay, okay!' I said, walking over to the porthole. 'Just keep calm. I'll open this porthole, and we'll **ALL RUSH YOU**.'

I looked back at Spencer, Patrick and José, who were frowning at me.

'We'll **ALL RUSH YOU** when the porthole is open ... I mean, **all rush through**,' I said.

'O'Malley, my patience is wearing thin,' said Kurt Remarque.

I was out of time, but I felt sure the others had got my message. I grabbed the handle on the side of the round window and pulled. At first it wouldn't budge, but then as I hauled with all my strength it gave way and the window swung open.

'NOW!' I yelled, rushing in Kurt's direction.

This was it! With all four of us racing towards him, Kurt wouldn't know what to do and we would have him in our power. I charged towards my fat white enemy, already imagining what it would be like to have my hands around his neck, wrestling him to the ground. **What a brilliant plan!**

After about ten steps I stopped. Kurt was looking at me as if I were an idiot. I looked behind me and none of the others had moved. They were all standing there like statues.

'What are you doing?' I yelled.

'What are **you** doing?' said Spencer.

'I'm carrying out the plan,' I said angrily.

'What plan?' said Patrick and Spencer together.

'Didn't you understand my brilliant code?' I said. 'When I said we **ALL RUSH YOU**, that was a sign that we should all rush him. **How much more simple could it be?'**

'I thought you said we **all rush through**,' said Patrick. 'I'm sure I heard you say we all rush **through**.'

'Yes, I heard that too,' said Spencer. 'Isn't that what you said?'

'Yes, but that was just to confuse Kurt Remarque.'

'Well, you certainly confused **me**,' said Spencer.

'Me too,' said Patrick.

'I am **really** confused, my friends,' said José.

'What kind of a stupid plan was that, anyway?' said Patrick. 'How did you expect —'

'ENOUGH!!' Kurt's bellowing voice echoed around the ship's hold as he stamped his foot. There was a **CREAK** of the boards beneath our feet.

'This nonsense has gone on long enough,' he said. 'I want you off this boat and I want you off **NOW**.' Kurt stamped his foot again, making his huge white belly wobble like a furry jelly. The boards creaked again, more loudly now.

I looked down.

There was a crack in one of the boards. Had it been there before? I wasn't sure, so I followed it with my eyes. It snaked along the floor for several metres, ending in a little gap in one of the boards — the gap where Patrick had pulled out his splinter. The gap was right near where Kurt was now standing.

'All right, we're going,' I said. 'There's no need to stamp your feet.' As I said this I stamped my foot as hard as I could and saw the crack creep another few centimetres across the floor. 'See? Stamping your feet never helped anything,' I went on, and stamped my foot again.

This time there was a much louder **CREAK** — followed almost immediately by an even louder **CRACK**.

We all looked at the floor — even Kurt — as the crack began to run the length of the boat. Right where

Patrick had pulled out his sliver of wood, a small puddle of water had begun to form.

'**Uh-oh,**' said Kurt.

Uh-oh indeed.

A huge jet of water burst through the floor as if someone had turned on a giant fountain. The force of the water pushed Kurt backwards and the gun flew from his hand.

'What's happening?' came Patrick's voice from the other side of the room. I could only just hear it over the sound of the water.

'We're sinking!' I yelled. 'Head for the porthole, quick. It's our only way out.'

The crack was heading crazily in all directions now as the hull of the boat came apart. I started pushing through waist-deep water to where the porthole window was swinging back and forth. Spencer and Patrick were both ahead of me, but I couldn't see José or Kurt.

There was a **THUD**, a groan and the sound of splintering wood. I looked behind me just in time to see the entire container-load of gold disappear through a gigantic hole in the bottom of the boat.

'NOOOOOOO!!!' My precious gold!'

The voice belonged to Kurt Remarque. He had clambered onto the top of the container, and the suction almost pulled him down as his treasure began to head towards the ocean floor. At the last minute he leapt across to the stairway that led up to the deck of the ship and swung precariously from the handrail. Then slowly he started clawing his way up.

Everything was happening very quickly now. In a matter of seconds, the water was over my head, and I felt myself swirling helplessly around. A flash of colour swept past me and I felt something grab my hand. It was José, swimming strongly and dragging me towards the porthole. Somehow we squeezed through it, and found ourselves out in the open water.

The boat was sinking fast and I was tumbling head over tail, trying to hold my breath. The water was filled with all sorts of debris — slabs of broken wood, barrels, bits of rope. Below me the ocean was dark, but I could just make out a slim shaft of watery sunlight from somewhere above me. I headed for it.

The water grew paler and clearer, and suddenly I was bobbing on the surface like a cork. A very scared, waterlogged cork. I took a deep breath and looked around. I couldn't see anyone.

'Ocko! Over here!'

I looked behind me and there were Spencer and Patrick, clinging side by side to a skinny little plank of wood. Rats are not the best swimmers — if you don't count water-rats — but I did my best to paddle over to where they were and grab hold of an edge of the plank.

'Are you two okay?' I gasped.

'Absolutely,' said Spencer. 'We've just been shipwrecked, we're clinging to a tiny piece of wood, and we're stuck in the middle of the ocean.'

'Apart from that, we're fine,' added Patrick.

'Good plan, by the way,' said Spencer.

I was just trying to think of something smart to say in reply when I noticed a tiny boat in the distance.

'Look!' I yelled. **'Over there!'**

It was the little rowboat that had been sitting on the deck of the ship. 'The captain and the sailors must have used it to make their escape when the boat sank,' I said.

I looked closer. I could just make out the figures of the sailors, pulling hard on the oars as they rowed to safety. The captain was sitting at the back of the boat, leaning on a couple of sacks. There was a small barrel on the boat, too — perhaps one of the whisky barrels — and ... and ...

'Look at the boat!' I said to the others.

'What about it?' said Spencer.

'There, at the back, next to the barrel. Can you see it?'

'See **what**?' said Spencer, peering into the distance.

'Something white — fat and white. It's right behind

the barrel there. The monkey people probably can't see it from where they're sitting.'

'I can't see anything,' said Spencer.

'Me neither,' said Patrick.

The rowboat was disappearing from view. The rest of the ship had sunk, leaving only a few bits of wood and an oil spot on the bobbing waves. I clung to the plank and gazed into the distance.

'You think it was Kurt, don't you?' said Spencer. 'You think Kurt was on that boat.'

'Maybe,' I said. 'Maybe. I just wish I could be sure.'

'Ahoy!'

'Ahoy?' I said to Spencer and Patrick. 'Did you hear someone say **Ahoy**?'

'It sounded like **Ahoy**,' said Patrick.

'Over here, my friends!'

The shout came even louder now. A wave lifted our plank into the air then gently lowered us again, and suddenly we could see a huge slab of wood heading in our direction. It was like a rough, badly made raft — five or six planks from the side of the boat fitted together with a piece of cross timber. Lying right in the centre of it, resting comfortably on a sack of `FINEST PERUVIAN WHEAT` , was José.

'Climb aboard,' he said.

So we did.

Things were pretty straightforward after that.

José proved to be an excellent sailor, especially after we tied his poncho to the plank and hoisted it into the air. It filled with air and began pushing the little raft through the gentle waves.

'The winds here blow straight back towards the Peruvian coast,' said José. 'My friends on the wharves have told me this many times. So we just relax and wait

and soon we will be home.'

And that's exactly what happened — although I can't honestly say that I relaxed at all. The trip took seven hours, and for most of the time I scanned the horizon, searching for signs of that little boat. But I saw nothing.

'What a waste,' I said. 'All that gold, all those treasures. Lost. Think of all the good we could do with that money.'

'Believe me, we are better off without it,' said José. 'The treasure of Atahualpa was a wonderful dream, a mystery. Far better to stay that way forever.'

'Anyway, look on the bright side,' said Spencer. 'The gold is at the bottom of the sea, along with whatever evil plan Kurt may have had for it. We're all safe and well, and Kurt's on the run. That means we win and he loses.'

'Maybe so,' I said, 'but I'd be happy if I knew where he was right now, and even happier if I had him under arrest.'

After a while I heard seagulls flapping and screeching above us, and then the loud blast of a foghorn.

'See!' said José, jumping to his feet and almost knocking the raft over. 'Beautiful Lima!'

The coastline of Peru was up ahead and several large container ships were moving in and out of the port. The wind carried our little raft sideways, away from the wharves, and we eventually washed up on a little sandy beach, not too far from the centre of town.

'You know, it's the sailors I feel sorry for,' said Patrick the Magnificent as we clambered off the raft and walked across the sand to the road. 'They must have got the shock of their lives when the whole ship started collapsing underneath them.'

'Never feel sorry for monkey people!' I advised him. 'They're mean and selfish, and they persecute every rodent they see. The fewer humans in the world, the better it would be!'

Spencer looked across at me as we trudged down the road towards town.

'Has it ever occurred to you,' she said quietly, 'that **mice** sometimes feel that way about **rats**? You push us around, you tell us what to do, and you treat us like second-class citizens.'

'That's the most **ridiculous** thing I've ever heard,' I said. 'You're just jealous because your brains are smaller than ours and you can't do everything we can do.'

I thought it was a very good point, but the effect was spoilt a little when I stepped straight into a pothole, fell headfirst onto the road and scratched my leg. It reminded me of how sore I still was after losing so much of my fur. Spencer and Patrick rushed over and helped me up.

'Stupid monkey people!' I said grumpily. 'They can't even build a proper road.'

Anyway, we kept walking. Eventually, we made it all

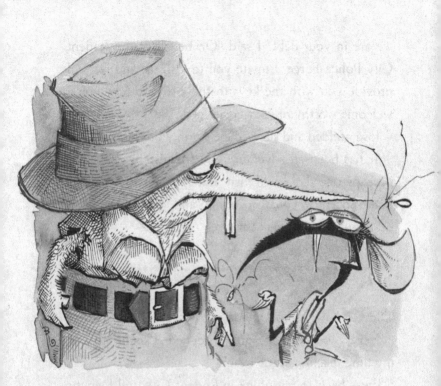

the way back to the markets of Lima, where we gathered a fine collection of cheese, bread and olives from the stalls. Then José led us through a small opening in a wall at the end of the alley, down a few steps, then through an even smaller hole, and we found ourselves safely back in his large, airy home.

The next day we were back at the airport, making our farewells before climbing onto a plane that would take us back to Rodent City.

Spencer and Patrick both hugged José. I shook his hand slowly and solemnly.

José Manuel Carlos Maria Pedro de Ollantaytambo,

we are in your debt,' I said. 'On behalf of the Rodent City Police Force, I invite you to visit us, and we will provide you with the keys to the city, and give you a welcome worthy of your great deeds.'

José nodded and slapped me warmly on the back.

'It has been an adventure, my friends,' he said, 'and perhaps one day I will visit. But for now, my place is here. So enjoy your trip home, and we will see each other again — of this I am sure.'

****

'Did you have a good holiday, sir?' said Deputy Smith.

'Very good indeed, Smith,' I replied. 'I spent most of my time relaxing at the beach.'

I was back in my office in Rodent City and Deputy Smith was filling me in on what had been happening while I was away.

'Six robberies, three burglaries, four mice arrested on suspicion of selling goods without a licence, and ten violations of the *Cheese Code*,' he said, reading from a long list in his hand.

'Sounds like a pretty normal couple of weeks,' I said. 'Anything else to report?'

'Oh, just this,' said Deputy Smith, waving another piece of paper under my nose. 'The Rodent City Council wants to close two streets tomorrow while they bring the crane in.'

'The crane?' I asked. '**What** crane?'

'For the building job,' said Smith.

'**What** building job?'

'Oh, of course,' went on Smith, 'all this happened while you were away. The Council has voted to put up a statue to Kurt Remarque, now that he has died.'

'A **statue**?' I said, grabbing the paper from his hand. 'Whatever for?'

'Oh, I don't know,' said Smith. 'Something about commemorating all the great work he did as one of the leading businessrats of the city. Mayor Boskin voted against it, for some reason, but all the other councillors supported it.'

I knew why Mayor Boskin had voted against it — he was the only other rat who knew how evil Kurt Remarque really was. I sighed.

'Oh well, Smith, I suppose Rodent City can always use another statue. After all, the pigeons need **somewhere** to sit.'

I leaned forward and tossed the paper on my desk, and as I did, Smith stared at my arm. 'You've lost some fur, Sir,' he said. 'Did you have an accident on holiday?'

'Ah, um, yes,' I said quickly. 'I was hit by a Frisbee. On the beach.'

'It must have been a big Frisbee,' said Smith.

'Huge,' I replied. 'Biggest you've ever seen.'

There was a knock at my office door.

'Just get that on your way out, will you, Smith?' I asked.

'Certainly, sir,' he replied, gathering his papers together. 'Oh, and ... welcome back.'

He opened the office door to let in my visitor. It was Spencer.

She strolled across the office and sat down in the chair opposite me.

'So, did you tell him?' she asked, picking up a pencil from my desk and twirling it around.

'No, I didn't,' I said. 'I thought about it, but what would be the point? I can't prove Kurt has committed any crimes, and right now I can't even prove he's alive.'

'Maybe he's not,' said Spencer. 'Maybe you just **think** you saw him on that boat. He could be at the bottom of the ocean right now, along with his gold.'

'You could be right,' I said slowly, rubbing my whiskers. 'Anyway, what brings you to my office?'

'Oh, nothing, really,' said Spencer, getting to her feet again and heading for the door. 'It's just that I'm planning another meeting next week of the Society for the Cooperation of Rats And Mice, and I was wondering whether you might like to come along.'

'What night?' I said cautiously.

'Tuesday,' said Spencer. 'The first item on the agenda will be the plans for a Rat and Mouse Festival this summer.'

'I'll think about it,' I said. 'I might be free, as it happens.'

'So, maybe I'll see you then,' said Spencer. 'Only this

time, cut out the bad jokes, okay?'

I was still thinking of a suitable reply as she opened my office door, and with a flick of her tail she was gone. The door closed softly behind her.

I stood up, walked slowly to my office window, and looked out over Rodent City. I was still a bit sore in a

few places, but most of my fur was growing back nicely. Things were returning to normal — but one thing just kept nagging at me.

I gazed over the rows of houses towards the distant horizon.

You're out there somewhere, Kurt, I said to myself. **I can feel it. You're out there and you're up to no good. And something tells me we'll meet again ...**

I picked up the phone on my desk, and rang for some doughnuts.

THE END

Alan Sunderland is the author of seven children's books and when he is not making up stories, he is the Editorial Director of the ABC. He has worked as a journalist for almost forty years, but never once met a detective who was a rat. He lives with his family in Sydney in a street called River Road, which also happens to be the name of a notorious mouse gang.

LOOK OUT FOR ...

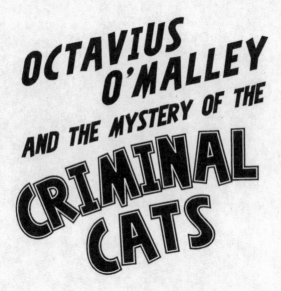
OCTAVIUS O'MALLEY AND THE MYSTERY OF THE CRIMINAL CATS

OCTAVIUS O'MALLEY
AND THE MYSTERY OF THE CRIMINAL CATS

Everyone knows that rats hate cats, but who expected things to get this bad? Gangs of cats roaming the streets, rocks falling from the sky, and a mysterious evil cult that OcKo and his gang need to investigate.

And what on earth is that terrible smell?

Stay tuned for the third adventure of Octavius O'Malley — the biggest and scariest one yet!